Praise for the Red Carpet Catering Mystery Series

"The Red Carpet Catering series delivers a buffet of appealing characters, irresistible movie-industry details, and tantalizing plot twists. As delicious as a gourmet meal—and leaves you hungry for more!"

– Susan O'Brien,
Agatha Award-Nominated Author of *Finding Sky*

"Movie lovers, this is your book! Engaging and high-spirited, Penelope Sutherland never expected that catering for the cast and crew of a top-flight movie would lead to...murder. Great fun."

– Terrie Farley Moran,
Agatha Award-Winning Author of *Caught Read-Handed*

"With a nice island flavor, a nice puzzling mystery and a great cast of characters, this was a very enjoyable read."

– *Dru's Book Musings*

"A fast-paced cozy easily read and enjoyed in an afternoon...with Simmons' picturesque writing style you can almost taste the salt in the air. Take a vacation and join Penelope."

– *The Reading Room*

"Such a fun book. The characters are very likable and the writing is very well-done. Think of it as a cozy behind the scenes."

– *Booklikes*

"Delicious! A great read written by someone who knows the behind the scenes world of filmmaking...A winner!"

– Kathryn Leigh Scott,
Author of the Jinx Fogarty Mysteries

"This series is so well done that you will feel as though you have just gone to a friend's house to visit for a few hours."

"Loved this book! The characters are well-drawn and it's cleverly plotted. Totally engrossing...I felt as though I was actually on a movie set. The author is well-versed in her setting and she is able to keep the reader in suspense. I can't wait for the second book in the series."

"Much of what makes this such an enjoyable new mystery is the background information on both catering and movie-making. Equally compelling is just how seamlessly author Simmons works Penelope into the investigation...this is a fun new series for readers who enjoy their theatrical showbiz mysteries with a culinary twist."

"A fun mystery on a movie set and delightful chef with delicious sounding food....Shawn Reilly Simmons has a flair!"

"With a likeable cast of characters and an inside look at the movie industry, this was equally entertaining and engaging."

"Simmons has given us quite a good beginning to a new series; she manages to create characters that are both believable and likable while weaving in small tidbits of movie-making and what is involved in catering food to a movie crew...Highly recommended."

MURDER
WITH ALL THE
TRIMMINGS

The Red Carpet Catering Mystery Series
by Shawn Reilly Simmons

MURDER
WITH ALL THE
TRIMMINGS

A RED CARPET CATERING MYSTERY

SHAWN REILLY
SIMMONS

HENERY PRESS

For Colleen Shannon, my biggest cheerleader

ACKNOWLEDGMENTS

I've always wanted to write a mystery set during the holidays, that magical time we get to spend appreciating our families. And of course, all of the great food that comes along with them!

A theme that runs throughout this series of books is family, the ones we're born into and the ones we create throughout our lives. I'm very lucky to have a supportive family of my own that is a constant source of support and comfort along this writing journey, as well as the mystery writing community, my created family, that is always there to offer guidance and encouragement. It's often said that writing is a solitary profession, but I've never felt more included within a large family than I do right now.

I'm also grateful for Kendel Lynn, Art Molinares, and Maria Edwards, and everyone else at Henery Press, for their constant championing of my books. Their enthusiasm and encouragement means the world to me.

And thanks again to all of the readers out there. You keep me going, and I can't thank you enough.

And as always the biggest thanks goes to Matt and Russell, who help me believe that I can accomplish anything.

Love,
Shawn

CHAPTER 1

Penelope Sutherland stirred her peppermint mocha latte and stared out at the rush of holiday shoppers scurrying past the department store's café. Even though Christmas was still several weeks away, and it was a Tuesday afternoon, the Manhattan store was bustling with harried-looking shoppers. Penelope crossed her legs and rotated her foot around, releasing the tension in her ankle. She'd managed to finish almost half of her Christmas shopping already, picking up a few odds and ends in the kitchen and housewares section of the store that morning that she planned to give to her staff, the hardworking chefs she employed. She thought back to her first year as chef-owner of Red Carpet Catering and the homemade jars of brownie mix with red and green bows she'd tied onto them. It was what she could afford to give after paying out holiday bonuses and the premium on their health insurance plans.

At the register in the housewares department, Penelope ordered a set of top of the line, steel-clad pans for her sous chef, Francis. Francis stood shoulder to shoulder next to Penelope, cooking on the line from the very beginning. She felt a warmth spread in her chest when she handed over her credit card to the sales clerk, imagining his face when his Christmas gift arrived.

She blew on the surface of her coffee and took a sip, savoring the minty chocolate as it slipped across her tongue. Penelope was working on mindfulness, reminding herself to enjoy small moments, flavors, feelings and experiences, ever since spending time at the end of the summer on a movie set in Vermont. The director was a yogi and had urged them all to pay more attention to the world around them. Penelope hadn't agreed with everything he'd said, but she did see the value in pausing to enjoy life's simple pleasures.

Shoppers stepped quickly past the doorway of the café grasping different sized packages and bags, the iconic name of *Steiners* in golden script across the red and green foil. An older man in a rumpled overcoat paused near the entrance and squinted at the menu over the counter, his arms ladened down with gift-wrapped boxes. His expression was pinched, as if trying to decide if he had time to stop. His gaze fell to Penelope and she offered an encouraging smile.

"Do you know where the handbag department is? I thought for sure the woman downstairs said it was up here on the seventh floor," the man said, lifting the corners of his mouth in an exasperated smile. He glanced at her oversized purse slung across the back of the chair, which Penelope guessed gave her some inside knowledge of the department store's layout.

"Second floor, I believe," Penelope said, pointing at the floor. "This is all housewares, kitchen stuff up here. Women's is on two, Menswear is on three." She guessed she knew more than she thought about Steiners, after all. She had been coming to the store since she was small, with her mother most of the time. She remembered buying her first formal dress here, back when she was sixteen.

"Are you sure?" the man asked.

"Yes, I'm almost positive," Penelope said gently. She wrapped her hands around the paper cup in front of her.

The man sighed and his shoulders sank. "Okay, thanks," he muttered and gave her a tired smile before scuffling away. He was out of earshot before Penelope realized he was heading in the opposite direction of the escalators and would have to backtrack to get down to where he wanted to be.

"Here's your Buck Noel," a young woman said, thunking a box on the café table in front of Penelope. She wore a green felt elf costume complete with a pointed hat, which drooped toward her face. A fluffy white ball bounced in the center of the black frames of her glasses.

"*Buche de Noel,*" Penelope corrected her.

The elf sighed. "Isn't this what you ordered?" She looked down at the shiny gold box that was shaped like a log.

"Yes, it's right," Penelope hurried to say. "It's just you said 'buck' so...it's a French pastry. It's pronounced *Buche.*"

The girl shrugged her shoulders dismissively. "Can I get you anything else?" She tapped her foot that was encased in a red felt moccasin. The toes of them curled up toward her ankles and sported more poofy white cotton balls.

"No," Penelope said. "I send my mom one of these every year for Christmas. They don't have Steiners stores where they moved. Down in Florida."

The elf glanced back at the line forming at the counter. A young man dressed in a matching red elf costume took coffee orders and pulled pastries from the case beside the register. "That's nice. I should probably get back to help with the customers."

Penelope smiled. "Right. Sorry. Happy Holidays."

The elf snorted a laugh and stuck a hand on her hip. "That's a good one. I'll be happy when my shift is over. I've never seen so many people in here."

"You work here all year?"

"No, I'm seasonal help." The elf stomped away, avoiding eye contact with the people waiting in line as she ducked back behind the counter.

"There you are," a familiar voice said from the café entrance.

Arlena Madison, Penelope's best friend and roommate, strode over to her table. She had on a white cashmere coat, a wave of her sleek black hair spilling over her shoulder. She took the seat opposite Penelope and set one of the store's large green shopping bags on the floor, then peeled off her white leather gloves.

"Did you find what you were looking for?" Penelope asked.

"I wish," Arlena said. "I still have a few things left to get. I found this for Max." Arlena craned her neck and looked at the line that now stretched almost to the store entrance as she pulled a long thin box from the bag. She opened it and revealed a black and tan plaid Hermes scarf.

"Oh, he'll like that. That's just his style," Penelope said. Max was Arlena's half-brother, the sibling she was closest to from their father's many children.

An espresso machine steamed behind the counter. "I'd love a cup of tea, but the line is so long," Arlena said.

"Everywhere is busy it seems," Penelope said. "And it's not even Thanksgiving yet. The shopping season is so rushed now."

"I know," Arlena said. "But I have the time now, so I figured I'd get a head start. I'm trying to shake the perception that I'm a procrastinator."

"Did you find anything for Randall?"

Arlena rolled her eyes. "What do you get a man like my father who literally has everything?"

Several of the tables around them began to fill up with people taking a break from shopping to sip a coffee or nibble on a croissant.

Suddenly the elf reappeared at Penelope's side. She set down a large paper cup of hot water and a few teabags in front of Arlena.

Penelope and Arlena gazed at her as her cheeks reddened. "Um, I hope you don't mind. I'm a big fan."

Arlena smiled. "Well, thank you. I'm always happy to meet a fan. How did you know I prefer tea?"

"I read that about you in an article once. I assumed it wasn't fake news."

Arlena smiled. "It's a fact, I prefer tea. Always have."

A few people in the line turned to watch the exchange, interested but wary glances on their faces, ready to call foul if the elf strayed too long from her duties behind the counter. Penelope could see a few of them recognized Arlena, but being typical New Yorkers, they wouldn't acknowledge they did in order to maintain their "seen it all" personas.

"Could I get your autograph? I've seen all your movies," the elf stammered. She swiped at the fuzzy ball that was perched in the center of her dark framed, hipster glasses and pulled a pen and store napkin from her apron.

"Sure," Arlena said. She spread the napkin on the table and signed it carefully, so as not to rip it. "What's your name?"

"Chamaya," the elf said. Arlena glanced back up at the elf and raised her eyebrows in question.

"C-H-A-M-A-Y-A. I graduated from Anderson, the performing arts high school two years ago. I'm auditioning for everything I can now. I'll take anything at this point."

"That's great," Arlena said, scrawling on the napkin.

"Do you have any tips for someone like me, just starting out?" Chamaya said, biting her lip. A man in line behind her cleared his throat loudly. Penelope glanced at the elf behind the counter, who was hustling to keep the line moving.

Arlena handed the napkin and pen back to Chamaya. "The best advice I can give you is to stay positive, go after the roles that interest you, and don't do anything you feel goes against your values. Stay true to yourself and don't compromise your principles to please others."

"Wow, thanks," Chamaya said, staring down at the napkin. "It's hard getting the rejections. You know. Well, you kind of had the door opened for you, with your dad and everything. Being from the Madison family you probably didn't get the door slammed in your face like the rest of us."

"Excuse me, miss?" the man from the line said. "Do you mind? Some of us have places to be."

Chamaya ignored him. "Thanks, Arlena, for your encouragement."

Arlena shook her head. "Anytime. Good luck to you."

Chamaya stepped back behind the counter and the man behind them sighed with irritation.

"I found the perfect gift for you," Penelope teased, taking a sip of her drink.

"Oh yeah?" Arlena asked, dunking her tea bag. "What's that?"

"A really nice silver platter just like the one your career was served up to you on," she teased. "It matches the silver spoon that was in your mouth when you were born."

Arlena rolled her eyes and laughed. The line began to move more quickly, and Penelope felt the tension in her shoulders ease. Even when she was enjoying a break, she always found herself observing food service workers around her, resisting the urge to jump in and help.

"Yeah, well, we all know life's been one big cake walk for me," Arlena said, nodding.

"Speaking of cake, I got my mom's *bouche de noel*," her eyes flicked to the gold box on the table. "Now I just have to find something for my dad, and something perfect for Joey."

"And what are you thinking of getting for your handsome detective boyfriend?" Arlena asked slyly.

Penelope hesitated, then pressed on. "I'm not sure yet." Penelope hadn't told Arlena that she and Joey had been looking off and on at houses in their neighborhood in New Jersey, and that she was contemplating moving out of the home they shared. In reality it was Arlena's house. Penelope lived there and worked as Arlena's personal chef. Although they had become such close friends, their roles of employer and employee had blurred at the edges. Arlena was like the sister Penelope had never had.

"I was really working on getting my shopping out of the way before the Big Apple Dancers project starts up," Arlena said.

"Me too," Penelope said. "We still have a few more days before we have to be on set, right?" Penelope glanced at her phone, checking the date.

"It's weird calling the theater a set," Arlena said. "Do they call it a set when it's a documentary?"

"I wouldn't think so," Penelope admitted. She drained the last of her latte and wiped her lips with a napkin. "It's my first one. We'll have to learn all the differences between a documentary and a fictional movie."

"A learning curve, my favorite. It's also my first time working directly with Daddy." She placed a slender knuckle against her red painted lips and stared at Penelope. "What if this turns into a nightmare?"

Penelope crossed her arms at her waist and thought for a second. "It's not going to be a nightmare. Your dad loves you more than anything."

"Yeah, but working with family...I don't know." Arlena said, tapping her knuckle against her chin. "I couldn't say no to him, of course. So it's a moot point. Max too. We want to make him happy, especially after all he's done for us."

"There's that silver spoon again," Penelope teased.

Arlena set her mouth in a line.

"I think it's exciting," Penelope said, reassuringly. "The Madison acting clan coming together on a project about the Big Apple Dancers. I never knew your grandmother was one of them."

"Daddy had mentioned it a couple of times when I saw him growing up," Arlena said. "But we never really talked about her a lot until recently."

Penelope cleared her throat and brushed a few crumbs from the table. "Do you feel weird talking about it? I know things were hard sometimes, you know with your dad not being around."

"No," Arlena said. "He's around now, with a vengeance. I would've liked to have met my grandmother, though. Too bad she passed away before I was born."

"Well, maybe this way you'll get to know her a little better," Penelope said.

"I think that's why I said yes to this project so quickly. Learning about my grandmother, well, that was too hard to resist. I'm glad you'll be there with me." She leaned over and motioned for Penelope to lean forward too. She rested a cool hand on top of Penelope's on the table. "I know I have sisters out in the world. Probably quite a few of them, knowing Daddy. But you'll always be the closest one to me."

Penelope blushed and flicked her eyes to the table. "That's so sweet. I feel the same."

"So, we should head over soon," Arlena said. "Thanks for meeting me here. I know you're busy, but I wanted to get that scarf."

"I love Steiners, and I got some things too," Penelope said. "It wouldn't be Christmas without a walk through the store."

Arlena looked down at her half-empty cup and then at the counter. The line had dwindled to just a few people, with the two elves slowing their pace during the brief lull.

"Ready to go?" Arlena asked. "We're supposed to meet the director soon."

"Yeah," Penelope said. "Let's do it."

CHAPTER 2

Penelope and Arlena's boot heels tapped the sidewalk as they made their way up New York City's bustling Fifth Avenue. They walked at a brisk pace, in keeping with the crowd around them, pausing a few times on their journey to admire the elaborate holiday display windows of the different shops and boutiques they passed. They had to dodge around a tourist or two, unused to the rapid flow of pedestrians on the avenue that had come to a dead stop in the center of the sidewalk, pointing their camera at a building or take a selfie in front of a famous address.

Penelope and Arlena stopped when they came to a window where a small crowd had gathered. A little girl in a pink winter coat and matching earmuffs pointed at the glass as she tugged on her mother's hand.

A couple dressed as Santa and Mrs. Claus were in the display window. Mrs. Claus tipped back and forth in her rocking chair as she knitted a pair of tiny elf leggings. Santa was in a matching rocker, rubbing his swollen belly with one white gloved hand and grasping a yellowing scroll of paper in the other. Santa's list pooled at near his black boots on the floor, presumably with scrawled names of naughty and nice children on it.

"I think he saw me," the little girl whispered to her mother, who smiled and nodded.

"This is the best time of the year to be in the city. I can't wait to watch the parade," Arlena said after they'd begun walking again.

"Me too," Penelope murmured.

"You seem a little off today. Is everything okay?" Arlena asked as they paused at the next corner, waiting for the light to change. A yellow cab whizzed by on the cross street, blowing its horn for some reason.

Penelope shook her head and smiled, tugging her dark purple knit hat over her ears, her long blonde hair streaming across her shoulders. "I always miss my parents more this time of year."

Arlena stepped closer to Penelope and their shoulders touched. "Why don't you invite them up for the holidays?"

"I don't know," Penelope said with a shake of her head as they crossed the street. A van inched toward them, the engine revving in anticipation of the light turning green. "I'm not sure how much time I'd have to spend with them. We're going to be busy with this new project."

"Pen," Arlena said as she dodged around a woman pushing a stroller, "there's a billion things to do in New York during the holidays. They're originally from New Jersey, right?"

Penelope shrugged and nodded. "Yep."

"Look, it's Christmas, family time. Our house is more than big enough for them to come and stay as long as they like. Please, just think about it."

"Okay, I will," Penelope said. "But they'd probably want to stay at a hotel. They'd feel like they were imposing at our place."

"Well, that's silly. They haven't even met Joey yet," Arlena said. "It's time they got to know your boyfriend. They should come. For a lot of reasons."

When they arrived at the next corner, they turned and walked down the street, stopping halfway down the block in front of the Vitrine Theater. A few homeless people were huddled under coats and blankets, bundled up against the cold wind several yards away from the door. The smell of cigarette smoke and body odor mixed with stale liquor wafted over to them.

Arlena and Penelope climbed the slate steps and Arlena pulled on the theater's heavy wooden door. When it rattled against the deadbolt, she reached over and pressed the buzzer on the doorframe.

After a moment a fuzzy voice called over the speaker. "Hallo?"

"It's Arlena Madison," she said into the speaker.

"Oh yes, be right there!" the man's said quickly.

Arlena stepped back from the door and gave Penelope a shrug. But Penelope could tell she was excited to have arrived at the historic site.

The door opened and a man leaned out, glancing up and down the sidewalk briefly before saying, "Welcome, Miss Madison, please come in."

Arlena and Penelope stepped inside the darkened theater, and the man closed and bolted the door behind them.

"You certainly are Randall's daughter. There's a clear resemblance," the man said. His silver hair was swept up in a gravity defying swoosh, and a burgundy and gold scarf was tossed over the shoulders of his charcoal-colored wool suit. A small diamond stud twinkled from one of his earlobes. "I'm Armand Wagner," he said with a slight bow. "And you are Arlena Madison, who needs no introduction." His eyes shifted to Penelope.

"This is Penelope Sutherland. She'll be assisting me and providing catering for the crew and performers during the documentary filming."

"Oh wonderful," he said cheerily. "We're very happy to have you here for your project. And I must add your father's donation to the theater was very much appreciated. It certainly came at a good time and kept the wolves from the door, as they say."

Arlena smiled. "Well, when he heard there were some..."

"Financial troubles," Armand replied helpfully. "My dear, it's been in all the papers we were considering Chapter 11."

"Right," Arlena said, clearing her throat. "When he heard that, he just felt it was right to step in and help."

"Help? My dear, he saved us from a possible forced bank sale. Who knows who might've taken over this place and turned her into lord knows what? A coffee shop or a tattoo parlor? Midtown is prime real estate for anyone of course. They wouldn't care about our history." Armand's smile went all the way to his eyes. "But now, the tradition of the theater will carry on into the future. A few more years, at least."

"So, you're the director?" Arlena asked, peeling off her gloves.

"Artistic director. Yes. For as long as I can remember," Armand said with a faint laugh. "Since the mid-eighties, when you were just a girl, I assume."

"I see. So far, I've only worked with film directors," Arlena said. "What's the difference?"

"Less cameras, for one," Armand said. "But there are similarities too. I oversee the creative direction of the theater, and all the projects and plays we produce. Of course, our biggest event of the year is the Christmas Extravaganza. People come from all over the world to see our show and the Big Apple Dancers. We're a holiday tradition for thousands of families. Come, let me show you around."

Armand led them through the foyer past a vintage ticket booth with gold-etched glass windows. A brass tray on the counter, worn from years of theater goers sliding money and tickets back and forth, glowed in the dim overhead lighting. Penelope pulled off her glove and touched the cold metal, imagining what it must have looked like when it was brand new.

Armand flipped a switch on one of the walls behind a heavy red curtain, and the overhead lights brightened, highlighting the dust motes they'd disturbed by opening the door and letting in the frigid air. On the left of the main room was a large wooden bar with shelves lined with liquor bottles in front of a gold-rimmed mirror that matched the ticket booth.

"Please, let me stash your things in the coat check so you'll be more comfortable." Penelope and Arlena shrugged out of their coats and handed their shopping bags to Armand. He put their coats over his forearm and carried their things through a door, the kind where the top half swung open and created a small counter. Penelope imagined a coat check girl leaning there in a pillbox hat, like the ones she'd seen in black and white movies on the classic film channel.

"And this," Armand said after closing the door to the closet and waving them forward, "is where the magic happens." He ushered them through a set of double doors and into the main theater.

"Wow," Arlena said, gazing up at the four half-circle seating balconies lining the walls. Everything was draped in gold and burgundy, the same colors as Armand's scarf. He moved easily down the aisle, his long slender body moving like a dancer's, his familiarity with the space around him obvious.

"The girls will be here soon," Armand said over his shoulder as he strode toward the massive stage.

"This place is amazing," Penelope said under her breath to Arlena. "It looks a lot smaller from the outside."

"The magic of the theater," Arlena whispered.

Armand ducked behind the curtains on the left-hand side of the stage. A few seconds later the stage lights flipped on and the curtains rolled slowly apart to reveal a set designed to look like a winter wonderland. An oversized sleigh attached to a cluster of animatronic reindeer glittered with artificial frost. Snowflakes of all different shapes and sizes dangled from invisible wire overhead, and stacks of brightly colored gift-wrapped boxes dotted the stage.

Armand stepped out to center stage and took a quick bow in their direction. "The Christmas Extravaganza opens this weekend. We always time our debut each year with the Steiners parade, when the city's holiday tourist season really gets going."

The muffled sound of the front door rattling open caused Penelope to turn away from the stage and look toward the lobby. The curtains separating the entryway from the lobby swayed gently from the rush of outside air, and a woman appeared at the top of the aisle.

"Armand!" she shouted. "My girls are standing outside freezing. Why didn't you let them in?"

Armand took another bow, this time with a flourish. As he straightened up he said, "Martha, my dear. No one rang the bell. How was I to know they were waiting?"

The woman took a few more steps across the carpet and eyed him suspiciously. "Are you having a private party in here? Who are these women?"

Armand crossed his arms and shook his head. "No, Martha, of course I am not having a party. They are theater patrons, Arlena Madison and her associate, Penelope Sutherland."

"Because we don't have time right now for your schmoozing if we want to rehearse enough for this show. My girls need to practice every minute they can!" Martha said, eyeing Arlena up and down.

"By all means, bring them in, Martha," Armand said with a roll of his eyes. "Arlena, if you wouldn't mind, I've so much more to show you."

Martha stepped back through the curtains and shortly afterwards they could hear many voices, chatting and laughing together as they entered the theater.

Penelope followed Arlena onto the stage at Armand's urging.

A stream of young dancers flooded the aisle, laughing and talking with each other as they moved as a group toward the stage. They were all roughly the same height—taller than average as far as Penelope could see—and all with similar body types: slender and long-legged. There were about thirty of them, many with gym bags thrown over their shoulders, wrapped in jackets, scarves and coats. Penelope watched them climb the stage steps and head toward a door behind the curtain on the left. A couple of them threw glances at Arlena and Penelope as they passed.

"Ten minutes to get changed, darlings!" Martha shouted, ushering them like a mother hen through the door. "I want to see all of you on the stage warming up in eleven minutes from now."

"Welcome to this year's crop of Big Apple Dancers," Armand said after the last one had passed through the door into the dressing rooms. "And our head choreographer, Martha Shirlington."

"Lovely young women," Arlena said.

Armand nodded crisply. "Of course they are. Part of the job requirement is to be lovely and graceful. Please, if you'd follow me.

Martha's been in charge of the new class for twenty years now. She never fails to whip them into shape."

Penelope pressed a hand to her stomach, which was relatively flat and toned, especially considering she spent most of her time at work cooking and tasting food. Even though she was fit compared to most, she could tell these women were as fit as they come.

Armand led them through a matching door to the one the dancers went through stage right. On the other side was a darkened space filled with set pieces and a wooden staircase that led straight up, wrapping around three different landings on the way. The air around them smelled of plywood and dust and the steps creaked beneath their feet. When they reached the top, Armand led them into a small waiting room. A set of mismatched visitor chairs lined the walls, and black and white photos filled every space above them. Penelope looked closer at a few of them, recognizing the stage below and what looked like different productions the theater had put on over the years.

They made their way through another door into a smaller office where Armand took the seat behind a heavy wooden desk. Penelope thought about the rickety staircase and wondered how anyone could have gotten that desk up there.

"Sit, please," Armand said, waving at two vintage leather chairs. "And tell me, what will you need from us, the Vitrine staff, to make this project successful?"

Arlena cleared her throat. "The first thing that comes to mind...I'd love to interview you, and Martha as lead choreographer. It would be great to have your input on the theater's history, and any insight you can provide on this place. I'm sure you've experienced many things our viewers will find fascinating."

Armand folded his hands together on the desk and grinned. "Well, of course. We're happy to. What subjects will you be focusing on, do you think?"

"Well, we want to highlight the history of the place, but also touch on a few personal histories, anything compelling that you think would make a good story. Something that ties in with the history, things that have happened here over the years that may have influenced the way you do things here today."

"Oh how fun!" Armand rubbed his palms together and smiled. His skin was smooth, almost as if it belonged to a much younger man than what his shock of silver hair suggested. He picked up a gold pen and twirled it in his slender fingers as he leaned back in his chair.

"We'd like to interview a few of the dancers, too. Get their take on what life is like as a Big Apple Dancer."

The pen paused in his fingers and Armand glanced at his hands. "Yes, we should be able to arrange that. I'll run the idea past Martha...it will probably have to be before or after rehearsal. She's strict about them not missing stage time."

"You said Martha's been here twenty years?" Penelope asked.

"Even longer than I have," Armand said with a shake of his head. "Where do the years go?"

"We don't want to disrupt the production, of course," Arlena said. "We're aiming for an observational documentary, so the less intrusive we are the better. We can talk with them whenever works best."

"And you've brought your own caterer," Armand said, eyeing Penelope curiously. "Do you have any experience working in a theater, my dear?"

Penelope smiled and shook her head. "Not professionally, but I've been here before, many years ago now. My parents took me to see Big Apple show few times as a kid."

"Oh brilliant!" Armand said.

"Until now I've worked on movie sets," Penelope said. "When I was starting out I did a few commercials, a music video one day."

"Hm," Armand said. He pressed a knuckle to his lips and studied her. "The main difference between a long running theater production and a television show or film is we do the same show every day, over and over for weeks. You'll see after a while you can set your watch by what's happening on the stage. Precision, that's our motto."

"I'm certain we can adjust to whatever needs Arlena and the crew here might have," Penelope said confidently.

Armand leaned forward and laced his fingers on his desk. "When Randall said he had a young chef acquaintance who would be on hand during the filming, I just assumed..."

"Assumed?" Penelope asked.

"I assumed, because he said the chef owned their own company and had worked on major productions, he was referring to a man."

Penelope smiled. "I'm happy to surprise you."

"And I'm happy to be surprised!" Armand exclaimed suddenly.

Penelope paused a second before speaking again. She heard Arlena laugh under her breath. "So, what do you normally do catering-wise for the cast and crew here?"

"We have a snack table backstage, sandwiches, you know the ones that come in plastic wrap, that kind of thing. When I heard you were coming, I figured I'd wait before diving into any deli ordering," Armand said.

"How many people are we talking about each day?" Penelope asked.

"Roughly 150. That's counting the dancers, stagehands, Martha and her choreography team, the set builders, orchestra musicians, the costume department, massagers, the hair and makeup team..." Armand stared into space as he ticked items on his fingers. "Anyway, it's a big show with lots of crew, but that's the rough count, I'd say. I'll make sure to show you the facilities and introduce you both around to everyone."

"I assume women in the shape those dancers are in stick to some kind of regimen and diet," Arlena said.

"I'm sure I wouldn't know. In my day," Armand said, waving to a photo on the wall behind them, "it was cigarettes and oranges in the morning, not much else during the day, then a thick steak at Sardi's once a month on payday."

Penelope glanced at the photo behind her of a young Armand, standing in the center of the stage, his arms over his head, mouth opened wide in song. His hair was just as voluminous, but jet black, in what Penelope guessed by his costume was sometime in the 1970s.

"Those were the days," he sighed.

A brass buzzer sounded from the corner of Armand's desk and he shook his head. "Rehearsal is beginning. Would you care to observe?"

"Oh we'd love to," Arlena said.

Armand stood up from his desk and motioned for them to follow. He led them to a door behind the visitor chairs and pulled it open. On the other side was a narrow balcony.

"Come, take a look," Armand said, leaning over the railing.

Penelope stepped out behind Arlena and walked cautiously to the end, aware of the creaking boards beneath her feet.

"Look there, they're lining up," Armand said.

Several stories below them Penelope could see the stage and the dancers getting into position. They weren't in costume, so it looked like an exercise class assembling instead of a troupe of Broadway dancers. Penelope felt slightly woozy when she looked down—the space between them and the stage yawning below.

"Line up!" Martha shouted and clapped her hands in a staccato rhythm. The dancers stopped their chatting and got into rows, shuffling in their high heeled dance shoes into the shape of an upside-down V.

"When the theater was built in 1895," Armand muttered, "the founder and creative director, Thaddeus Vitale, lived up here with his family. He had this balcony built so he could keep an eye on the plays from his home."

"Wow," Arlena said. "He raised a family up here?"

"Three girls," Armand said. "Two of them were actresses, which makes sense, I suppose. They grew up on the stage, literally."

"What did the third one do?" Penelope muttered.

"She wrote, as a journalist mostly," Armand said. "The mother died of typhoid when the girls were very young, all still under the age of ten. Mr. Vitale dated a string of actresses afterwards, women who were working on this very stage. Rumor has it he picked the ones who showed the most interest in his girls, like temporary mothers, you see. The youngest daughter wrote a book about the Vitale girls and their stand-in mothers."

"I'd love to read that book," Arlena said. "They sound like an interesting family. And it would be an enlightening historical angle for the documentary."

"Well, the book has been out of print for many years now, but you might still be able to find a copy somewhere," Armand said, gazing down at the stage. "I can also show you our archives. We've kept clips of articles, show bills, reviews, things like that. You are welcome to help yourself to anything you like."

Arlena balled her hands into fists and Penelope could sense her excitement, even with Armand standing in between them.

"Places!" Martha shouted. Her hair was pulled back in a severe bun at the nape of her neck, a thin black turtleneck sweater reaching up to meet it.

The dancers positioned themselves into two lines. When they were settled, there was a gap in the one on the left. Penelope swept her gaze around the stage and toward the dressing rooms, looking for someone who might be running late, but no one appeared.

"Where's Elspeth?" Martha asked. Several of the dancers shook their heads and shrugged.

"Elspeth!" Martha called. She tucked her hands on her thin hips, clad in close fitting black pants. "If you're not lined up in ten seconds we'll call in your backup!"

When no one appeared, Martha took a few steps upstage and craned her neck, somehow sensing they were standing above and gazing down at them. She raised her palms in the air and shrugged.

"Where is Elspeth, Armand?" she called into the space between them and the stage.

"I'm sure I don't know," Armand said.

CHAPTER 3

Martha called another performer to the stage from the group of four backup dancers that were waiting on the sidelines.

"Those are the swings," Armand said, lifting his chin toward the group of women. They were dressed like the others, in spandex workout clothes. The one on the far left shifted her weight from leg to leg. The one next to her rose up and stretched her calves a few times.

"Swings?" Penelope asked.

"Stand ins," Armand said. "They're ready to take over a spot, any spot on a moment's notice in case one of the front lines can't perform."

"How are the dancers chosen?" Arlena asked. She kept her eyes on the stage.

"A very long audition season each summer. It takes years to get to the front line for some," Armand said. "Other times a girl will come straight off a bus from Nowhere, Iowa, and be that year's Snow Queen. That's the nature of musical theater. Talent is rewarded as its discovered."

Music drifted up from below. It was a familiar Christmas tune Penelope remembered singing with her mom while they made cookies in their old house in New Jersey.

"Shall we observe rehearsal from the seats?" Armand said.

"That would be great," Arlena said.

Armand led them back through the office, closing the door behind him as they entered the waiting area on their way to the stairs. Halfway through the room he stopped abruptly. "There," he said, pointing at a framed photo on the wall. "I told you I could see the resemblance."

The picture was of twenty or so dancers dressed in sparkly white leotards with short silky skirts and knee-high boots. Armand's finger hovered near the center, pointing at a beautiful woman with black hair and a radiant smile.

"Oh my," Arlena said, stepping closer to the wall. "That's my grandmother?"

"That's her," Armand said dropping his arm and clasping his hands behind his back. He took a step back to allow room for Arlena to move closer. "Ruby was the Snow Queen that year, the star of the Christmas Extravaganza."

Penelope eyed the frame and the gold plate that was fastened to it. The year 1937 was etched in the gold.

Arlena reached out a hand and went to touch the glass covering the photo, then pulled back at the last minute. She cleared her throat. "I never got to meet her. She died when my father was young. Do you have any other pictures from her year? It would be great for background material."

Armand nodded and motioned toward the door. "The archive has photos and other relevant items for each year. We've been working to digitize the oldest pictures so we don't lose them forever, but that's an off and on project, mostly handled by interns during the summer."

"Interns?" Penelope asked.

"Mostly theater students. They get credit for coming to help us, and they get to see what it's like behind the scenes of a working historic theater."

Penelope and Arlena followed Armand carefully down the rickety wooden steps, changing direction at two landings before arriving safely at the bottom. During their descent, Penelope willed herself to only look as far as the next few steps down. She thought anyone with a fear of heights or vertigo would not be able to manage this theater. Or at least work in Armand's eagle's nest of an office.

The music from the orchestra met them at full volume as they reached the bottom of the steps backstage. Armand led them through stage door right and down to the front row in the main seating area of the theater.

Penelope watched in awe as the dancers worked through their routine, moving in unison with each other, marching to a medley of holiday songs. Their legs were lithe and muscular, their abs taut behind their leotards. Most of them held their gaze at the horizon somewhere over Penelope's head, their faces fixed in toothy smiles. Low-heeled character shoes stomped and scraped against the boards as they worked their way through the number, all completely in unison, not one foot out of place, at least as far as Penelope could tell.

When the song ended, Martha stood up from her seat a few rows behind them and made her way to the stage, the stark blades of her shoulders pressing against her black sweater.

The women on stage eyed her approach nervously. One of the dancers bent over at the waist, visibly huffing and trying to catch her breath with her hands on her thin hips.

"You, move two back, everyone else step forward," Martha said. The dancer who was asked to take a downstage position fought to hide her disappointment. Without a word of protest, the company did as Martha asked.

"Once more from the beginning," Martha said. She mumbled something to the conductor before returning to her seat. His back to the audience, he tapped his stand and the music began again after a few beats. Penelope could only see the tops of a few of their heads but guessed there were a dozen or so musicians in the pit. The dancers once again moved in unison around the stage in perfectly formed lines, kicking their legs in time with the music. Penelope was not an expert in dance, but she was impressed by the display of apparent skill on the stage.

"Martha is very exacting," Armand mumbled. "She'll make them do it twenty times before opening curtain if she thinks they need to."

"Incredible," Arlena whispered. Her eyes followed the routine on the stage, and she tapped her boot on the floor in time with the music.

"The opening show is the Friday after Thanksgiving, and day one must be perfect," Armand said, nodding. "The press will be here, VIPs. We like the kickoff to help spread the word every year."

"Have you ever gotten a bad review?" Penelope asked.

Armand sucked his teeth quietly. "A few times," he admitted. "Before my tenure here," he hastened to add.

"This show is such a tradition," Penelope said. "Would a bad review keep people away?"

"It certainly doesn't help, my dear," Armand said. "And we need to watch the bottom line, as they say."

"What did the critic say?" Penelope said. "I mean, how bad could a Christmas show be?"

Armand chuckled. "People had different ideas back in the day. There was one director in the late sixties who thought making a political statement was the way to go. Some anti-war sentiment of his, definitely not in keeping with the holiday mood."

"Oh," Penelope mumbled. "Yeah, that's not good."

"Exactly," Armand said. "Theatergoers want to leave behind the outside world once they take these seats. They want to be transported to a beautiful place where dreams come true." Armand smiled widely and his eyes glistened.

"The magic of the theater," Arlena said under her breath.

"Quite," Armand said.

As the dancers appeared to be coming to the end of their first routine, the outer doors of the theater rattled open. Penelope glanced over her shoulder and saw a woman hurrying down the aisle from the lobby toward the stage. She paused and watched the dancers for a second, then headed straight for Martha.

Martha glared at the young woman, who wore a dark green peacoat over black yoga pants and shiny winter boots. The look of irritation on Martha's face softened as the woman knelt in the aisle and whispered something to her, then morphed to concern. Martha cupped the girl's cheek in her hand, then stood up next to her in the aisle, grasping her hand. The young woman began to cry, shaking her head as Martha attempted to calm her down.

"She's gone!" the woman shouted toward the stage.

Martha patted her upper arm, then shot a glance at the orchestra conductor who was watching them curiously.

"Let's take a break," Martha said to him as she led the woman toward the dressing rooms.

The music dribbled to a stop, the last sound from a violin bow dragging slowly across the strings. The dancers paused and watched in confusion as Martha urged her along.

At the last second, the woman broke from Martha's grasp and turned to the dancers.

"No," she said, her pale cheeks reddening beneath her tears. "She's gone. When did you see her last?" Her face was doll-like, her pale skin smooth and fragile.

"Abigail, let's talk this out. I can see you're worried, but I don't think it's as urgent as you think," Martha said. "Let's go figure out what's happened without disrupting rehearsal."

Armand stood up from his seat and put his hands on his hips. "Martha, what's the matter with the poor girl?"

"Elspeth is gone," Abigail said. Fresh tears began to flow, and her body shuddered as she hugged her torso tightly over her pea coat.

"What on earth is she talking about?" Armand asked. "Elspeth has missed rehearsal today, my dear, that's all. She'll probably get moved to swing unless she can provide a doctor's note. But it's nothing to get this worked up about."

"No, she's gone," the young woman insisted. "She never came home last night!"

Martha shook her head and gently took Abigail by the elbow. "Please, I'm sure she just decided to stay with someone, maybe with a friend?"

Abigail shook her head forcefully. "She doesn't know anyone besides us in the city." She looked at the other dancers on the stage who stood silently in their formation, eyeing her with concern. "And she would never just stay out all night without letting me know. She would text or something, wouldn't she? She's worked so hard to get here, she wouldn't screw it up by pulling a no-show and losing her spot on the front line. Something's happened to her!"

Penelope and Arlena exchanged glances. Arlena shrugged and adjusted the cowl of her cashmere sweater.

"Let's go sit down backstage and make some calls. We'll figure it out," Martha said. Her tone was gentler than Penelope had ever heard her speak before, but it was still no nonsense and firm.

Abigail shook her head and went to the edge of the stage and took a seat, her legs dangling into the orchestra pit. The musicians were all standing, watching her. The entire rehearsal had ground to a halt. A stagehand stuck his head out from behind the curtain and shrugged at Martha, tapping his watch.

"She's intimidated by the city. New York," Abigail said darkly. "It's overwhelming for her—the crowds, the filth. She would never stay out all night. Never. It's my fault, I should've gone with her." Abigail broke down in sobs.

"Go with her where?" Armand asked, standing up from his seat and moving into the aisle.

"To the store. Last night," Abigail said. She pulled her knees up and hid her face behind her hands, folding in on herself into a ball.

Two of the dancers knelt next to her, one of them wrapping her long arms around Abigail's shoulders.

Armand walked to the stage. "We're going to find her, my dear. Martha, do you think you can calm the poor girl down so we can find out what exactly is happening here?"

Martha nodded sharply and waved the other dancers away. "Take a break. But don't leave. We still have hours to go."

"Let's start at the beginning," Armand said gently to Abigail. "What time did you last see Elspeth, and what store are you talking about?"

"When we left rehearsal yesterday. She said she had an

appointment, and that she'd be back at the apartment by supper after going to get some groceries." Abigail paused, her voice breaking. "That was yesterday afternoon. She's been gone a whole day almost. We need to call the police!"

CHAPTER 4

"Maybe we should leave," Arlena mumbled to Penelope in the front row. "We've gotten a lot to start the project and they seem..."

Penelope nodded. "Yeah, they've got a situation to deal with." She and Arlena stood and shuffled between the seats toward the aisle.

"Arlena," Armand said, calling from the stage. "You don't have to leave just yet. We'll have this sorted out very soon."

"Oh, it's actually time for us to get going," Arlena said. "We very much appreciate your time today. We'll let you get back to," her eyes fell on Abigail, "whatever you need to take care of."

Armand stood in front of the sobbing young woman, still curled into a tight ball at the edge of the stage, her shoulders shivering beneath her coat.

"I hope everything turns out okay," Penelope called softly.

Arlena and Penelope made their way to the coat closet in the lobby to retrieve their things. As they got closer it was clear the door was ajar.

"I could've sworn I watched Armand pull that shut," Penelope muttered, reaching for the knob. The top half of the door swayed open and she looked inside. "Oh no, Arlena, look."

"What?" Arlena asked, alarmed.

"Someone's been in here," Penelope said in disbelief. "Our packages and purses...all of our things are gone!"

Arlena and Penelope stared at the rummaged through coat closet for a moment and Arlena sighed. "I guess it really is time to call the police."

CHAPTER 5

The police officer listened intently as Penelope spoke, the radio on her wide utility belt chirping with static every few seconds. She wore a heavy winter jacket and tall boots. Her partner, a skinny red-headed man was nudging a few of the coats hanging in the closet and peering on the floor behind them.

"I guess we shouldn't have left our things in there. We thought it was safe," Penelope said. There was an old keyhole on the bottom half of the door that Penelope could look right through. "Since we were all inside and the doors were locked..."

"We've had some problems in the neighborhood lately," Armand said, wringing his hands.

"What do you mean by that, sir?" the officer asked. Her voice was clipped, her brown skin smooth. The nameplate under her badge read Smythe.

"Ever since that homeless shelter opened up down the street, my patrons get accosted for change while waiting in line to enter the theater," Armand said, his voice dropping an octave. "Most inelegant, I must say."

"Uh huh," Officer Smythe said, eyeing Armand's expensive suit jacket. "Have you had any recent break ins?"

"Not that I can recall," Armand said. "There was a woman who said her mink stole went missing one night last season, but I assumed she was making it up as part of an insurance claim."

"Why would you assume that?" Officer Smythe asked.

"I'd heard through the grapevine the woman in question was having money problems," Armand said quietly. "Old money problems. You know. Divorce." He whispered the last word dramatically with a roll of his dark brown eyes.

Smythe's partner, a skinny red-headed man who looked like he should still be in high school, exchanged a glance with her as he stepped from the coat closet. "I'm going to take a look outside." He pulled his coat's zipper up to the top of his jacket and stepped through the doors. A cold blast of air snuck past him as he left.

Abigail hurried into the lobby, apparently recovered from her crying jag on the stage. "Officer, please. You have to help my roommate."

Smythe's shoulders tensed and her expression sharpened. "What are you talking about, ma'am?"

Armand chuckled a bit too harshly. "Officer, I assure you, it's probably nothing," he said. "Abigail here is worried because her friend didn't come home last night."

Smythe's expression relaxed and placed her hands on her belt. "How long has it been since you've seen her?" she asked.

Abigail sniffed and tugged at her coat. "When we left rehearsal yesterday. Around four."

Officer Smythe shook her head. "She has to be missing for at least forty-eight hours."

"Two days?" Abigail asked, throwing her arms to each side in frustration. "Awful things could be happening to her. She has to suffer through two days of torture before you even start looking?"

Smythe watched Abigail carefully. "What makes you think that's what is happening? Is there anyone in particular who would harm your friend?"

Abigail shrugged and dropped her gaze to the ground. "I don't know...but what if some creep snatched her off the sidewalk?"

The radio on Smythe's belt beeped and she pressed the button to respond. "Go ahead," she said, keeping her eyes on Abigail.

"...in the alley behind..." was all Penelope could make out through the static.

Officer Smythe turned her gaze to Penelope and Arlena. "Good news. My partner found some of your things in the alley out back."

"Thank goodness," Arlena said.

Armand clapped his hands together once loudly.

Abigail stood frozen to the spot, the look of pleading remaining on her face. "Officer, please, you have to help me find my friend."

"Let me get this situation under control first," she said, "and then I'll listen to what you have to say and see if there's anything we can do."

CHAPTER 6

Penelope and Arlena followed Officer Smythe around to the rear of the Vitrine Theater. A wrought iron gate with an intricate pattern of swirls at the top creaked back and forth in the breeze. On the other side of the gate was an alley that curved around to the back of the building.

Penelope could see her messenger bag lying on the pavement with some of the contents spilled out.

"Wait here one second," Officer Smythe requested, stopping them near the corner of the building. She stepped gingerly over to the shopping bags and purses strewn across the concrete.

Her partner stood gazing down at the discarded items. "I see two wallets, and there are phones here."

Officer Smythe shook her head. "That's weird. What kind of thief doesn't take the wallets?" She pulled latex gloves from her pocket and slipped them on, knelt down and opened Arlena's purse.

"This bag isn't cheap either. Why would he go to all the trouble to swipe purses and leaves valuable stuff behind?" Officer Smythe said. "This purse alone has got to be, what...six hundred bucks easy?"

Arlena nodded. "About that, I think. It was included with the swag I got on a movie last year from the producers."

Officer Smythe stood up again and walked to the Steiners shopping bag on the ground. "Looks like they helped themselves to whatever was in here," she said, lifting the empty scarf box into the air. She waved Penelope and Arlena over. Her partner wandered farther away and stepped behind the far side of the theater, pausing every few steps to look behind large black cases that lined the stone wall that encircled the property.

"What are these for, you think?" he asked, touching one as he passed. They looked like oversized suitcases, some with white marker scribbled along the sides. Penelope could read CHRISTMAS EXTRAVAGANZA on a few of them.

"They're for transporting set pieces," Smythe said. "Props, things like that."

When her partner gave her a questioning glance she said, "My brother used to pick up work down here, unloading trucks for the theaters. He got paid by the hour, easy money."

He nodded and continued poking around the cases near the wall.

"Can we take a look and see what might be missing?" Penelope asked.

Officer Smythe nodded, and they gathered up their things, both of them looking inside their purses first.

"My wallet is here," Arlena said. "And my phone."

"Maybe not for the phone," Smythe said with a twist of her lip. "They're harder to break into now if you have a passcode. Which you always should have. Leaving the contents of the wallet behind...we don't see that every day."

Penelope thumbed through her own billfold. "My credit card is still here. I didn't have any cash on me. I spent my last twenty at Steiners getting coffee."

"So maybe our robber gained a conscience halfway through the job," Officer Smythe said. "It is the holidays, after all."

"Wait," Penelope said. "Something is missing."

"What?" Arlena said.

"I had a picture of me and my parents in here," Penelope said. "It's gone."

"Are you sure?" Officer Smythe asked.

"Yeah, I always keep it tucked back behind my license. Which is still here, but the picture is gone."

"Oh no," Arlena said. "The one of me and Sam from last

Christmas is gone too."

"You both carry photos in your wallets?" Officer Smythe asked.

"Not usually," Arlena said. "I just remember tucking it in there. It was one of those photo booth things. Sam ripped it in half, and I kept two of the photos. Sam kept the others. We're apart a lot so it was, I don't know, something for us to share."

"I've had that picture of my family in my wallet since culinary school, when I left home and then they moved away. I've always carried it," Penelope said. "My *Buche de Noel* is gone too."

"Your what now?" Smythe asked.

Penelope shook her head, then looked around the pavement, searching for the gold box. "It's a cake, a yule log kind of thing I just bought to send to my mom for the holidays."

"Okay," Smythe said. "You'll have to spell it for me for the report."

"Smythe," her partner called, "looks like someone's been living back here."

"Stay put," she said, nodding to her partner. "I'll be right back."

Arlena sighed and slung her bag over her shoulder. "It's always something in this city, you know?"

"I know," Penelope said. "I've never been mugged before. I guess there's a first time for everything. But why just take things that have value only to us?"

Arlena shrugged.

A gust of wind slipped through the alley, lifting one of the discarded shopping bags into the air. It landed against one of the set cases lined up next to the wall. Penelope hurried to retrieve it, stumbling against one of them in the process.

"Ouch," she said, rubbing her shin. The case lurched forward, and she reached a hand out to steady it, but instead lost her balance and stumbled back. The case fell on its side at their feet.

"You okay?" Arlena asked, grabbing Penelope's arm to help her regain her balance.

"Yeah," Penelope said, rubbing her shin harder. "That thing is much heavier than it looks." The silver handle of the case fell toward the ground and clacked loudly against the shiny black siding.

"What is in there that is making it so top-heavy?" Arlena asked.

The main latch popped open. Penelope put her hand over her mouth.

"Pen, get back!" Arlena called, pulling Penelope by the shoulder away from the case.

A woman with dark red hair lay face-down on the ground, her bare torso tumbling out of the set carrier. One of her arms was twisted beneath her, the other lay at an odd angle, her skin stark white against the cold gray concrete.

"Officer Smythe!" Penelope managed to choke out. She couldn't stop staring at the bluish tint of the skin on the woman's back.

Officer Smythe and her partner rushed over from the far side of the theater, coming to an abrupt stop when they saw the woman's body on the ground. Officer Smythe knelt down quickly and touched two fingers to the woman's neck. Her partner began talking into his radio, his eyes darting around the area near the body.

Penelope and Arlena took a few steps back, making room for them to do their jobs. Penelope thought they should turn away, but she was unable to take her eyes off the woman from the case.

CHAPTER 7

Penelope watched the EMTs from the other side of the police tape as they studied the scene. The man in charge had a black mustache and shook his head as his eyes traveled across her soft white shoulders and painted red fingernails. Officer Smythe's partner began to erect a tent to shield the alley from onlookers.

A van with a satellite dish on top of it double parked on the street next to where Penelope stood on the sidewalk. A woman with a heavily sprayed helmet of hair emerged from the passenger seat, a microphone with the letters CMZ gripped tightly in her fist. A tall man with a shoulder cam stepped from the back of the van and followed her to the sidewalk. The reporter turned her back to the alley and nudged Penelope lightly with her shoulder, jostling her from the shot. The man pointed his camera directly at the gate to catch as much as the police activity as possible before the tent was put in place.

"Okay, Bill, eyes on me," the woman said. She touched a manicured hand to her hair and cleared her throat. The man stepped back and pointed the lens at her. "This is Candy MacNamera for New York Four reporting live from the Theater District where the police have found the body of a dead woman at the Vitrine Theater. As of now the identity of the victim is unknown, but our police sources say foul play isn't out of the question. As you know, we're smack dab in the middle of the busy Broadway season, and it's not clear as of yet how this incident might affect ticket sales."

Penelope stared at Candy as she tossed back to the studio,

amazed at her flawless and smooth delivery. Candy MacNamera had been an entertainment reporter for News Four, the dedicated channel for all things New York, for at least the last fifteen years. Her voice was a familiar one, but Penelope had never seen her in person until now.

Candy dropped her mic and nodded to her cameraman. "Let's get some crowd reaction," she said. "Excuse me, miss?" Candy turned her attention to Penelope. "What's your name?"

"Penelope Sutherland," she said. She wasn't sure if she should say anything or not, then thought about what her dad always told her: *When in doubt, keep quiet.*

"What do you think about what happened here today? Any comment for our viewers?"

A wave of coldness ran through her as she locked eyes with Candy. "I don't have a comment," Penelope stammered.

Candy smiled encouragingly. "Can you tell us if you feel safe? Will you visit the theater district again after seeing something like this?"

"I...um," Penelope stammered. "I think..."

Penelope felt someone tug on her coat sleeve at the elbow and looked behind her. Arlena was standing there. She tilted her head slightly toward the theater, urging Penelope to join her.

"Arlena Madison!" Candy almost squealed. "Are you going to be in a play? What a scoop for our viewers. Did you know the dead woman?" The makeup on Candy's face reminded Penelope of stage paint, orange and pink swipes defining her prominent cheekbones on top of a sprayed-on tan.

"I'm sorry, Candy," Arlena said, pulling Penelope with her back up the theater steps. "Now isn't the best time for a comment."

"But, what connection do you have to the theater?" Candy pressed. "Should I call your father and ask him? I still have his number."

Arlena paused on the steps and turned back to Candy, a knowing smile on her face. "There is a connection to the theater," Arlena said. "Which will be revealed soon, at a more appropriate time. I'll have Daddy give you a call." Arlena and Penelope slipped inside the theater, Penelope stumbling slightly in the doorway before the door finally closed.

Once inside, Penelope's teeth began to chatter in earnest, and Arlena sat her down in the last row of seats in the theater.

"The press has caught wind of what's happened. Candy MacNamera specifically," Arlena murmured to Armand.

"Mr. Wagner," Abigail said, "what is happening? Where are the police?" She was huddled in a nearby chair, her knees pulled up to her chin, face puffy and voice scratchy from sobbing.

Martha had ushered the other dancers into the dressing rooms, and just a few of the musicians mingled near the orchestra pit, throwing glances up the aisles from time to time. Everyone appeared uneasy.

"I'm not sure what's happening for certain, my dear. A few belongings went missing from the coat closet, and they're investigating," Armand said.

Abigail looked at him with a confused expression. "Why would a reporter care about that?"

"Um," Armand said, rubbing his chin.

Officer Smythe came down the aisle, followed by a tired looking man in a black suit. "This is Detective Doyle. He'll be investigating the death in the alley."

"Wait," Abigail asked sharply, standing up. "What death in the alley?"

Armand turned to face her. "Something terrible has happened. The police are working to find out exactly what."

"Who are you, ma'am?" the detective asked, eyeing Abigail. His black hair was sprinkled with gray and his wool coat looked like it had seen more than a couple of winters.

"Abigail Hamilton. My roommate is missing," she said. "I told them...do you think—"

"I don't think anything, Miss Hamilton," Doyle said, raising a hand to keep her from continuing. "I've only just arrived."

"But you said there was someone dead in the alley," Abigail

insisted.

"Are you the one who found the body?" he asked. He reached into his pocket and pulled out a notepad.

"I'm the one who found her," Penelope said quietly from her seat. Arlena rubbed her shoulder and nodded.

"I'll know if it's Elspeth," Abigail said.

"Okay," Detective Doyle said with a sigh. "You two come with me. You," he pointed at Penelope, "so you can show me exactly what happened. And you," he nodded at Abigail, who stood in front of him, "to ID our victim. Possibly."

Penelope closed her eyes and nodded, then pulled herself up. She felt like an entire day had passed since they'd arrived at the Vitrine.

"Is there a back door to this place? The first set of vultures has arrived. I'd like to avoid them if possible." Doyle waved a hand toward the lobby, indicating the activity on the sidewalk out front of the theater.

"Of course, right this way, Detective," Armand said. His tone was casual but worry creased the corners of his eyes.

Penelope walked on stiff legs, following them down the aisle toward the stage. She hadn't fully shaken the jittery feeling that overtook her as she looked down at the woman's bare back, her fragile spine showing just beneath the skin, her arm twisted unnaturally on the ground. Penelope dreaded going out and witnessing it all again, but she knew she had to do whatever she could to help.

CHAPTER 8

"Be careful where you step," Detective Doyle said, pointing at debris on the ground in the alley behind the theater. They emerged from the back door and stood on the small metal landing. Three steps led down to the concrete below, but none of them made a move to be first to go.

"Please tell me again exactly what happened when you got to the alley," Doyle said to Penelope. She gave him the rundown of events, from following the officers behind the theater, to finding their things, to the case tipping over. Doyle listened carefully and nodded when she was finished. He waved for them to come down the steps, and head over to the tent.

A thin green sleeping roll and a shopping bag full of dirty clothes had been pulled out from behind the row of cases closest to the wall and placed near the tent in the alley. Penelope remembered the other officer mentioning someone might be living in alley, just before they found the woman in the case.

"I'm not sure I can do this after all," Abigail said. She stopped abruptly at the bottom of the steps and Penelope almost bumped into her from behind.

She turned back toward the door, and Detective Doyle placed a hand gently on her shoulder.

"This will really help, if we can get a positive ID sooner than later," he said. "It won't take long."

"But what if it is Elspeth?" Abigail said, tears threatening to spill again.

"Then I will immediately begin working to find whoever did

this to her," Detective Doyle said. "You can really help her by doing this."

Abigail nodded and steadied herself before ducking into the tent. Penelope stayed near the steps, just able to see the woman's arm and a spill of red hair on the stretcher inside. The woman's arm was delicately thin, the skin papery. Her palm faced up toward the sky, her dark red nails looking like drops of blood on the sheet. Penelope saw something faint on her wrist, a drawing or a tattoo maybe. Feathers, or a bird's wing, possibly.

Arlena had offered to come with Penelope to the alley, but she'd told her that she was fine. And also to hurry up and finish up whatever she needed to so they could leave soon. She wanted to go home, curl up under a blanket on her couch and drink a glass of wine. Or two. She'd had enough of the city, and definitely the Vitrine Theater for one day.

The sound of Abigail's cry stiffened Penelope's spine. One of the EMTs had pulled back the sheet that had been draped lightly over the dead woman's face. Abigail staggered and leaned into Detective Doyle. He gingerly tucked an arm around her shoulders, steadying her. Penelope took a few steps closer and gazed at the woman's face. Her mouth sagged open and her eyes were open and glazed over, staring at nothing.

"It's her," Abigail cried. "It's Elspeth."

Penelope pressed her hand to her mouth and closed her eyes, as she listened to Abigail's sobs. She knew that sound, and the image of the dead girl's face would stay with her for a long time.

Elspeth had been beautiful, but her cheeks were hollow. The dark red lipstick, the same shade as her nail polish had lost its sheen, and flaked from her lips. There was a smear of blood on her chin, and her left temple. Penelope wondered if it was hers or if maybe she was able to get a swipe or two at her attacker and it was his. She had faded bruises on her left cheek and a darker ring of them around her neck.

Penelope tried to picture the struggle Elspeth had been through. She wondered who harbored that much rage, and what could have possibly triggered someone to unleash it on this promising young dancer.

"I know this is difficult," Detective Doyle said softly. "But is there anything else you can think of that might help us? Any ideas about who might have done this?"

Abigail shook her head. After a nod from the detective, the EMT pulled the sheet back over her face, and then unfurled a large black body bag. He motioned for his partner to help him get it around Elspeth's body.

"Where are her clothes?" Penelope asked. "Was she completely naked?"

"Yes," Doyle said darkly. "We haven't found anything yet." He rubbed the back of his neck and looked at Abigail. "Do you remember what she was wearing when she left the theater yesterday?"

Abigail bit her lip as she stared at her friend's face. "Jeans, I think. And a green sweater she borrowed from me. Boots. She wore her dance gear to work but she usually threw an outfit in her bag when she had something to do after rehearsal. So she wouldn't have to go upstairs and change."

"Upstairs?" Doyle asked.

"There," Abigail said, pointing toward the street in front of the theater. Doyle led her from the tent and they rejoined Penelope at the stairs.

"You live right across the street?" Detective Doyle asked, motioning at the tall apartment building visible above the theater's rooftop.

"All of us do," Abigail said.

Doyle sighed.

"What's wrong?" Penelope asked.

"Nothing," Doyle said with a weak smile. "It's an extra layer of possibilities, now. Someone might have known where Elspeth worked, or where she lived."

"Or both," Penelope said.

"Or it's a random creep and it wouldn't matter where she

danced or lived," Abigail said.

"Maybe," Doyle agreed. "Tell me again what Elspeth's plans were when she left the theater yesterday."

Abigail closed her eyes and sighed before continuing. "She said she wanted to get some errands done, she didn't say exactly what, then come home and make dinner."

"Did Elspeth cook a lot at home?" Penelope asked.

Abigail shrugged. "I guess. She liked to cook. We have a small stove and oven. A mini fridge."

"A lot of people rely on take out dinners in the city, because the apartments are so small," Penelope said.

"That gets pricy," Abigail said. "And the food is fattening. Elspeth said she had to control what went into her body, and who knows what a restaurant is doing to their food."

Doyle glanced at Penelope then turned back to Abigail. "What kinds of errands do you think she was doing?"

Abigail shrugged again. "Dry cleaning, maybe? Food shopping. We didn't get into the details."

"So you guys are pretty close, I take it," Doyle said.

Abigail paused, then nodded. "We auditioned together and made the Vitrine troupe. We've lived together for two months."

"And how long did you know her before then?" he asked.

"We didn't. We met at the end of the summer, in auditions."

Doyle squinted at her. "So you could say you're new friends, then?"

"Yeah," Abigail said, a bit defensively. "It happens in this business. We bonded right away. This job, and lifestyle...you know what, you wouldn't understand."

"Try me," Doyle said.

Abigail's chin jutted slightly and her gaze hardened. "It's different, dancing for a living. You sacrifice. Relationships are hard. Not every man wants to be with someone who has to focus on their work more than anything else."

"Lots of people have difficult jobs," Doyle said. "What makes yours different?"

"We do three shows a day sometimes, and we're up on stage until our legs can barely move anymore." She crossed her arms across her chest. "And it's not just physical pain, there's the mental pressure too. Weighing yourself every morning, squeezing your swollen feet into your character shoes, overcoming the stress and pain, making it through one more number. Then you watch your friends go out all night and eat and drink whatever they want, go out on dates, act normal, go away for the weekend. Splurge. We can't do any of that. Me and Elspeth, we bonded over that shared experience of being driven. And being on our own."

"It does sound like a lot," Doyle said. "But you know what you're signing up for, right?"

"I told you," Abigail said. "You wouldn't understand what it's like, to have a dream, and then have that dream try and take you down night after night."

"Detective," Penelope said, shifting the subject. "How exactly did Elspeth die? I saw the marks around her neck."

"We'll know more after the official autopsy," he said evasively.

"She was strangled," Abigail said. "Obviously."

"But where did the blood on her face come from?" Penelope asked.

Doyle sighed, and seemed to debate with himself whether to tell them anything more. "It appears she was also stabbed."

"Stabbed?" Abigail whispered, crossing her arms.

Detective Doyle cleared his throat. "Did Elspeth have a boyfriend? I know you said the two of you didn't date much but...it's a big city, lots of opportunity to meet people."

Abigail shook her head emphatically. "No."

"How about you?" Doyle asked. "Seeing anyone lately?"

"Not since I was at home," Abigail said. "I broke it off with him when I got to New York. He couldn't take the pressure of my career."

"You and Elspeth were only friends for a short time," Doyle said. "Maybe there was someone from her past she didn't mention?"

Abigail looked at him, her expression hardening. "We live in a studio apartment," she tilted her head in the general direction of the street. "She wasn't seeing anyone. I would've known. We spent most of our time together."

"But there were some times you were apart," Doyle said.

"Not many," Abigail said. "We both danced here. She was on the front line and I'm swing. I go out on auditions here and there but honestly...we were best friends. This is all a shock." Abigail's eyes glassed over and she put a fist to her lips.

Penelope put a hand on her shoulder and squeezed.

"I understand. And I'm sorry for your loss," Doyle said. "But it's possible, is it not, for Elspeth to have...entertained someone while you were out at an audition?"

Abigail shrugged. "I suppose. But I think she would've mentioned it at least."

"Where are you from originally?" Doyle asked.

"The Oneida Lake area," Abigail said. "North."

"Okay," Doyle said. "Thank you for your help. Both of you."

"You think you know what Elspeth was like," Abigail said, nodding toward the tent, "but you don't. She was here following her dreams. She wouldn't have thrown it all away on some guy. The Elspeth I knew wouldn't be out all night, that wouldn't have been her choice."

"Sometimes people get to this city and leave their old lives behind," Penelope said gently.

Abigail shook her head. "No. Not her. She worked too hard to get to where she was."

CHAPTER 9

After the EMTs wheeled Elspeth's body away and eased her into the ambulance, Abigail and Penelope followed Detective Doyle back inside the theater. Abigail headed to the dressing rooms, mumbling that she had to use the ladies room.

The rest of the Big Apple Dancers were gathered in small groups around the stage, talking quietly with each other. Armand and Martha stood at one end of the stage, matching expressions of anxiousness on their faces.

Arlena sat in the first row, her chin propped on her fist as she jotted notes on a small pad in her lap.

"Can you show me Elspeth's dressing room and locker? I'd like to take a look at the common areas also," Detective Doyle said.

"Of course." Martha waved him over and lead him through the curtain. "All the girls are out of there, except Abigail."

"Let's give her a minute," Doyle said. "Ladies, were any of you close with Elspeth Connor?"

Several of the dancers shook their heads. A few remained still, looking like they were thinking about it. One of them raised her hand halfway.

"You knew Elspeth well?" Doyle asked.

"Um, not well," the woman said. Her dark ponytail spilled over one of her shoulders, and she stroked it as she spoke. "We shared a dressing room. She was nice."

"Did you know her before your time together here?" Detective Doyle asked.

"No," the woman said, rubbing her nose. "Just from the show."

"Did any of you do anything with Elspeth outside of the theater? Go for coffee or a drink?"

The dancer with the ponytail tucked one long leg behind the other and propped a fist on her chin, thinking. "We went for a coffee once. Just to the place down the street."

"Great," Doyle said. "What did you guys talk about over coffee?"

She bit her lip, then said, "How hard it was to stick the pivot turns in the third number."

"The what?" Doyle asked.

The dancer dropped her ponytail and put one foot in front of the other and turned her body around to face the rear of the stage, her feet staying in place. She turned back to face Doyle and shrugged. "We practiced in the coffee shop."

"I see," Doyle said. "Did she mention a boyfriend?"

"Maybe," the woman said. "It was a while ago, though. I can't remember exactly. I just remember she didn't know the name of the move I just showed you. But she knew how to do it."

"Is that unusual?" Doyle asked.

The dancer threw a glance toward the curtain just as Martha reappeared from behind it. "Yeah. Especially if you've been to dance school, like she had."

Doyle sighed. "Okay, so you think maybe, she might have been seeing someone."

"Oh yeah," the woman said with a quick nod. "We're all seeing someone." Martha gave her a stern look and the dancer's cheeks reddened.

"Only," Doyle said, "we heard your line of work doesn't allow much time."

"That's just an excuse if you want to get rid of a guy," she said with a laugh. "Junie over there is married. We're not robots, Detective."

"What's your name?"

"Robin."

"You from around here?" Doyle asked.

"No, I'm from LA, actually," she said.

"How long have you been in the city?" Doyle asked.

"A year next month. I've never gone a week without a gig, dancing in musicals. I'm not one of the ones who have to wait tables between jobs," Robin said with a small sniff and rub of her nose.

Martha spoke up from her place beside the curtain. "It's okay to come back now, Detective."

"Is it okay for us to leave?" one of the dancers called out from the group on the stage.

Detective Doyle sighed and said, "Okay, yeah. Thanks for your help. Not you, Mr. Wagner. I still have some questions for you."

Armand smiled and nodded. "Of course, Detective."

Abigail and Doyle went back to the dressing rooms and Penelope followed the other dancers off the stage.

"I think I'm free to go, too," Penelope said.

"Good, that's enough excitement for one day," Arlena agreed. "Armand?" she called to him.

Armand hurried down the steps and took Arlena's hands in his.

"We're going now," Arlena said. "Please call me if there's more I can do to help with anything," she waved a hand toward the stage.

"I apologize for such a dramatic first day," Armand said. "What you must think of us now."

"You couldn't help what happened," Arlena said. slinging her purse over her shoulder. "I'm just so sorry about the poor girl. I hope they figure out who did this."

"Yes, it is tragic," Armand agreed. "Martha is beside herself with worry for the girls already and then to have something like this."

"If you think we should table our documentary plans..." Arlena began.

"No," Armand said. "We shall proceed as planned."

"Will Elspeth's death delay the show?" Penelope asked.

"The extravaganza will go on as planned," Armand said quickly. "We have six sold out weekends, beginning this Friday. We can't disappoint the fans."

"That's only a few days from now," Penelope said.

"And we'll be ready," Armand insisted. "You know what they say. 'The show must go on.'"

CHAPTER 10

The next day, Penelope woke before the sunrise. She stared into the darkness of her bedroom, then closed her eyes and toyed with the idea of going back to sleep. Elspeth's face flashed through her mind, her lifeless eyes and the dark bruises at her throat. Penelope pushed the image away and focused on what had to be done that day in order to be ready for Thanksgiving. She had shopping to do, and she really wanted to get a replacement *buche de noel* for her mom. It was their tradition to eat one for breakfast the Friday after Thanksgiving, and make their Christmas lists together over coffee. She could still picture her mom slicing off pieces of the cake and dipping it into her hot chocolate at the kitchen table. It was their welcome to what her mom called the real Christmas season.

Downstairs in the kitchen, Penelope pressed the button on the Keurig machine, then turned on the light over the stove. She wasn't ready for the brightness of the overhead lights just yet. She unplugged her iPad from its charger next to the refrigerator and swiped it open, setting it on the island counter with her coffee, and a pen and paper from the island drawer. She slid up on a stool and began making her lists.

She started with the guests, Arlena and her boyfriend Sam Cavanaugh, who was supposed to be arriving later that day after being away for over a month on a film set in Toronto. She jotted down Max's name and a question mark next to it. She never knew who Max would show up with, it all depended on who he was dating at the moment. Penelope ran through the faces of the young actresses and non-actresses who had at one point or another been connected to Max, until they began to blur together. Randall Madison, Arlena's father would be joining them along with his steady girlfriend, Sybil Wilde, who they had all met on a film set in Indiana. They'd met her son and daughter, too, who had also worked on the film. Penelope smiled, as she jotted their names down.

She knew what Jackson and Dakota liked to eat, or at least what their mom had allowed them to eat, because she was the chef on their movie.

And last but not least, her and Joey would be spending Thanksgiving together.

Penelope sipped her coffee, cruising through recipe sites on her iPad and making a few notes. After she'd gotten her ideas together, she made another cup of coffee and pulled New York Four's website.

BIG APPLE DANCER FOUND MURDERED was the headline. She scanned through the article, noticing Candy MacNamera's face in a video window halfway down the page. She recognized the outfit from the day before, a hot pink blazer over a low-cut silk blouse. Candy began to speak wordlessly as the ticker ran across the bottom of the window. Penelope hit the button to turn on the sound and listened.

"...no suspects yet in the Big Apple Dancer's murder. The police are asking people to come forward, anyone with information, should call the tip line listed on your screen."

Penelope perked up when she heard Candy say "...a possible connection to the actress Arlena Madison. Arlena was here at the scene and was one of the individuals who discovered the murdered dancer's body."

Penelope sat up straight on her stool and clicked the volume up once.

"Miss Madison had no comment for the press, but she confided off the record the police were onto a suspect, and that she was sure all the facts would be revealed soon. We can only hope she is right, and that the killer stalking the theater district is found soon and brought to justice. And stay tuned for news of the Madison's Broadway debut, father and daughter on stage together. What a treat that will be."

The video ended and a circular arrow spun on Candy's face, re-looping the clip to the beginning. Penelope clicked off the site and set the iPad down, shaking her head.

"Where does she get this stuff?" Penelope murmured.

She opened a different news site that she trusted to have more accurate information. Scanning, Penelope found a short piece mentioning Elspeth's murder at the Vitrine Theater.

Abigail was quoted in the article as being Elspeth's best friend and roommate. Penelope scoffed at that a bit, since in reality the girls had only met a few months before. Armand wasn't mentioned by name, but the article quoted the Vitrine's director as saying they didn't anticipate any delays for the Christmas Extravaganza. The article went on to say tickets were still available for shows during the holiday season. Penelope frowned and shut down the iPad and rubbed her eyes with the heels of her hands.

Penelope sat and thought about Elspeth for another moment, about how she wouldn't be celebrating the holidays with anyone. Draining her coffee, Penelope considered her mug, then decided she'd have one more. The sun had begun warming the light in the kitchen, and she thought about its warmth as she turned from the coffee maker back toward the island.

Catching a glimpse of a shadowy outline of someone standing on the other side of the kitchen door, Penelope jumped, sloshing coffee onto her socks and the kitchen floor. She instinctively gripped the mug tighter and danced her body away from the hot liquid, just missing dousing the front of her pajama top.

"Sam!" Penelope said with surprise.

Sam Cavanaugh, action movie star and Arlena's significant other, waved at her from outside. The sun was just beginning to rise, so his face was still in shadow with an orange glow surrounding his head. He smiled and held a finger up to his lips in a "shh" gesture.

Penelope rolled her eyes and stepped around the puddle of coffee, setting the mug on the counter. She went to the back door and opened it.

"You scared the crap out of me, Sam," Penelope laughed. From Arlena's side of the house she heard Zazoo, Arlena's Bichpoo, yip behind the closed bedroom door.

"Sorry," Sam said with a wide grin. "It's a surprise," he added.

"I'll say," Penelope said. She walked to the sink and pulled several paper towels from the roll beneath the cabinet. "I thought your flight wasn't getting in until this afternoon."

"The director has a jet," Sam said, looking down the hallway toward Arlena's room. "He gave me a lift."

"You flew here on a jet?"

"No," Sam chuckled. "I'm not a real pilot. That was just a role I played in that movie. I hitched a ride with him to New York."

Penelope kept her expression neutral. "Nice to have friends in high places," she joked.

"Right," Sam said, not getting the reference. He set the suitcase he'd been carrying down near the coat rack by the back door. "I'm going to go surprise Arlena. We haven't seen each other in a month."

"I know!" Penelope whispered excitedly. "She'll be thrilled." Penelope bent down to wipe up the coffee from the floor and pulled off her wet sock.

Sam disappeared down the corridor and Penelope heard the soft click of the outer door of Arlena's suite of rooms. A moment later she heard Zazoo's barking and muffled laughter from Arlena. The door opened again and the little dog came scurrying out, sitting up on his hind legs and tapping Penelope's knee with his paw.

"Kicked out of the love suite, I see," Penelope said.

Zazoo cocked his head and stared at her, then made his way over to the little velvet doggie bed in the corner of the kitchen.

More laughter came from the direction of Arlena's suite and Penelope sighed. She took her coffee upstairs to get dressed and begin her day.

CHAPTER 11

Since Penelope wanted to replace the stolen Christmas treat from Steiners, and have it delivered to her mom in Florida by Friday, she decided to hop the train into New York and head back to the department store. She thought she might look for a few other gifts while she was there and make one more stop on the way home.

There was a different pair of elves in the café that morning, just as frazzled as the ones the previous afternoon, but they were quick and efficient, and within a few minutes she was on her way, an identical gold box under her arm. She treated herself to an eggnog latte in a to-go cup and headed to the customer service desk on the top floor.

Penelope dropped her gift off with the shipping department, including a handwritten note letting her parents know she missed them, and inviting them to come to her home for Christmas. On her way out of the store, she bought a box of imported chocolates and a holiday tea collection, tucking them into her bag before stepping back onto the sidewalk and hailing a cab. It was still early in the day and several were hovering outside the main doors of the store.

The cab sped down Broadway in lighter than usual traffic, which thinned even more as they headed toward the East River twenty blocks south. Penelope paid the fare then stepped out, tossing her empty coffee cup into the trash can in front of the bodega on the corner. She headed down the familiar street, pausing halfway down the block in front of one of the old brownstones. She looked up at the second story windows and saw a woman looking out, an infant over her shoulder. She rubbed the baby's back and bounced lightly on her feet. Penelope smiled and pressed on, past the courtyard and up the steps of the neighboring house. She pressed the buzzer and waited on the stoop, peeking through the glass outer doors into the small foyer.

The inner door opened and a woman peered out. When she saw Penelope, her face broke into a grin and she hurried to open the doors, waving her hand to usher her inside.

"Penelope Sutherland," Mrs. Sotheby said. "What a surprise! Come in, my dear."

"I'm sorry I didn't call," Penelope said. "I thought I'd take a chance you were home."

Mrs. Sotheby was a retired middle school teacher, so she assumed she'd be home. Penelope pulled the two gift wrapped boxes from her bag and held them out to her. "I got you and Sinay a little something from Steiners."

"You are so sweet," Mrs. Sotheby said. "Come in and sit. Sinay is at school...she'll be sorry she missed you."

Mrs. Sotheby led Penelope into the kitchen, where she took a seat at the table. Penelope had met the woman and Sinay, her foster daughter, the year before when Arlena's brother Max had been involved in an incident that happened in the house next door. Penelope had kept in touch with them, and always tried to visit when she was back in the area in between movies.

"Well, we'll get together again soon," Penelope said. "I'll be in town through the holidays. I'm catering for a documentary being filmed in the Theater District."

"Coffee?" Mrs. Sotheby asked. She opened a bakery box and set it on the kitchen table.

"No thanks," Penelope said. "I've had way more than usual already today."

Mrs. Sotheby patted Penelope on the shoulder and sat down. "You say you're working at a theater?"

"Yes, the Vitrine," Penelope said. "The Christmas show there. Arlena's family is making the movie."

Mrs. Sotheby rubbed a finger under her chin. "That

sounds...nice."

Penelope selected a croissant from the box and tore off an end. "Have you ever been to the show?"

"Oh, yes," she said. Her hair looked a touch greyer than Penelope remembered, but her eyes were bright and clear, and she smiled easily, as usual. Except for that moment.

"Is something bothering you?" Penelope asked.

Mrs. Sotheby shook her head and smiled. "It's nothing. It's just that my husband took me there when we were dating. I had such a lovely time with him, all during that few months we were courting. After he passed, I went to one of the Christmas shows with my reading group, but it was hard for me to enjoy it...I was thinking of Richie the whole time."

"I'm sorry," Penelope said.

"It's okay," she said. "It's been forty-five years now. He was killed not far from that part of town, in fact."

"I imagine it doesn't get easier," Penelope said. "You mentioned he died in a robbery at a store?"

Mrs. Sotheby nodded. "Yes, he had stopped in to buy me some flowers on his way home, and..." Her eyes misted over and then she shook her head. "But you know, I'm lucky to have Sinay now. And you." She put a soft cool hand on top of Penelope's.

"I see you have new neighbors," Penelope said, nodding her head in the direction of the courtyard.

"I do," Mrs. Sotheby said, perking up. "Lovely family, with a new baby. He does something in finance. She's some kind of internet person...I don't know what that is. But long story made short, she can work from home. But they do have a nanny come too. Clearly they're well off."

"It's nice to see a happy family over there after everything that happened."

"Yes," Mrs. Sotheby said. "Nothing like a baby to brighten your mood, make you think about the future."

Penelope left a little while later, giving Mrs. Sotheby a hug on the front stoop before heading back toward the avenue. She caught a glimpse of the woman next door sitting on a lounge chair in the courtyard, her baby wrapped in a blanket asleep in her arms. Penelope waved and the woman smiled then tilted her face to the sun.

CHAPTER 12

Penelope hopped into her Jeep at the train station back in New Jersey and drove out to a local farm that advertised free-range Thanksgiving turkeys. She picked up a bird big enough to feed their group, running through the list of names in her head one more time. She watched the turkeys peck the ground in the pasture while the owner counted out the bills she handed him. The birds appeared to be in good health and their environment was clean. Happy turkeys made for delicious dinners, she knew from experience. The farmer helped her tuck the dressed turkey into the cooler she'd slipped into the back of the Jeep before leaving that morning.

The farm was a good way out from where they lived, and Penelope enjoyed the scenic drive back and the warmth of the morning sun through the windshield. When she got back to town, she stopped at her favorite organic supermarket to gather the rest of their dinner.

"Sheesh," she said under her breath as she pulled into a parking spot near the edge of the lot. It looked like half the town was there, stocking up for the big day.

Penelope nudged her shopping cart around shoppers who were examining green beans one by one and turning sweet potatoes over and over in their hands, looking for any flaws on the outside. Penelope grabbed four handfuls of string beans, shoving them into a paper bag she'd taken from a nearby stack. A half hour later, her cart filled with everything she would need, Penelope headed to the checkout lines, which, while a bit longer than usual, were moving pretty quickly. As she stood in line and did one last sort through her basket, her phone buzzed in her bag. Penelope plucked it out and glanced at the screen.

She had three texts. One from her mother: *Sorry we're not spending Thanksgiving together, but we hope you'll come visit us in the spring! Big birthday for Dad, you know. He surprised me with a holiday cruise for Christmas! We're going to Spain! Love You Talk Soon.*

The next one was from Arlena: *Hey! Sam got here early! Where are you?* Penelope rolled her eyes and smiled.

The third was from her sous chef Francis: *Happy Turkey Day tomorrow, Boss. See you Friday. LMK if we need to order anything special for the first day of work.*

Penelope inched her cart forward in line.

"Excuse me." A woman with wiry grey hair approached Penelope, eyeing the items in her cart. "How do you make those?"

She was pointing at the two heads of purple cauliflower Penelope had perched on top of her pile.

"The same way you'd make the regular kind," Penelope said with a smile.

"Oh," the woman said, gazing at Penelope's cart. "You like interesting food."

Penelope took a closer look at the woman and noticed the buttons on her coat were off, she'd missed one, which made her coat hang unevenly. She wore slippers and what looked like pajama bottoms under her coat.

"Ma'am?" the cashier said, waving Penelope forward. The woman stepped up with her, as if they were together. The cashier eyed her carefully.

"Mother," a young woman called from a few rows over. "Mother!"

"Shh," the older woman said, ducking down a little. "I'm playing hide and seek."

"Are you okay, ma'am?" the cashier asked. Penelope couldn't decide if he was asking her or the woman next to her.

"Mother," the woman's voice was right behind them. "Time to go."

"Drat," the woman said with a sly smile. "She found me again. Nice meeting you."

Penelope looked back over her shoulder as she began loading groceries onto the conveyor belt. The young woman who had been calling for her mother took her by the elbow and led her to another aisle. She was wearing a long puffy coat that had salt stains around the bottom and well-worn boots that looked like they might be too big for her.

The cashier began dragging her items across the window and weighing her produce, the machine blipping away as her purchases added up. Penelope watched the numbers on the screen out of habit. When she was shopping for a production, she usually had to stay within an assigned budget, and the habit was hard to turn off.

Penelope paid for her items and placed the canvas shopping bags in her cart.

"Can you try it again?" the young woman's voice said.

Penelope thanked her cashier and pushed her cart toward the exit, pausing when she noticed the older woman and her daughter's pained expressions as they stared at the screen above the register. A small frozen turkey, a few sweet potatoes, and a box of cornbread mix were waiting on the conveyor belt to be bagged up.

"Try it one more time," the daughter said. She glanced at the man waiting in line behind them who was both trying to ignore them and suppressing an irritated glance.

"I'm sorry, it's declined," the young girl at the register said. Her tone was apologetic as she handed the card back to the young woman, who looked on the verge of tears.

"Here, I've got it," Penelope said, digging in her purse. She pulled out her wallet and handed the cashier her debit card. The cashier paused for a moment, then looked around for anyone to confirm it was okay.

"Go ahead, it's fine," Penelope said, holding it out to her again.

"Okay, whatever you say," the young girl said.

"Thank you so much," the daughter said. She pinched the bridge of her nose and took a breath.

The receipt sputtered from the machine and the girl handed it to the woman. Her mother beamed at Penelope as the cashier handed back her card.

After they'd placed their items in their cart and made their way out of the checkout lane, the daughter said, "We can't thank you enough. Please, give me your address so we can mail you a check."

"Oh, that's okay, don't worry about it," Penelope said. "It wasn't that much."

"I'd have to insist," the woman said. Her skin was dry and red, like she'd been out in the cold too long. "We don't expect charity."

"It's just a pay it forward moment," Penelope said. "For the holidays."

"She said she'd pay for it," her mom said through her yellowed teeth. "Let's scoot!"

"Mother!" the woman sighed. "Please at least give me your email. I can contact you that way to pay you back."

"It's really not necessary, but okay, here's my card." Penelope handed her one of her business cards with her email and cell phone number. "Happy Thanksgiving."

Before they could mention paying her back again, Penelope hurried away, sliding out through the automatic doors and back into the overcrowded parking lot.

CHAPTER 13

The morning of Thanksgiving, Penelope woke up early, the excitement for the holiday not allowing her to sleep one more minute past five. The night before she and Arlena and Sam had ordered takeout from their favorite Peruvian chicken place and had turned in early. Penelope because she knew she had a big dinner party to put on the next day, and Arlena and Sam because they were making up for a lot of lost time.

Penelope pulled the turkey from its brining liquid in the refrigerator and patted it dry, then buttered the whole bird and stuffed fresh herbs under the skin. She had the big guy in the oven by six, and her mouth began to water thinking about the roast turkey smell that would be permeating the air in just a matter of hours.

Next she set about baking her pies. Although she had graduated culinary school as a savory chef, Penelope still loved to bake, especially during the holidays and on special occasions. It was a different skill and mindset all together, and she'd studied alongside pastry chefs who she couldn't match when it came to gravity defying works of spun sugar art, but she could still cook a mean pie and please a crowd.

When her pumpkin and apple pies were in the oven, Penelope pulled out her prep list from the kitchen drawer and began making notes, crossing off items. Next up were the sides, so she sorted through the fridge and pulled out all of her veggies and pantry items and set to work.

*   *   *

"Hey, there she is!" Max Madison stepped through the back door. He was ladened with a shopping bag decorated with pictures of wine bottles in one hand and a large pastry box in the other.

"Hi, Max," Penelope said. She had just come back downstairs after taking a shower and drying her long blonde hair, which she had up in a ponytail. She'd pulled on jeans and a black V-neck sweater for their casual Thanksgiving Day dinner. The kitchen was humming along nicely, and everything was on target to be on time and perfect. "Ooh, Ferrara pastry!"

"Yeah, it's Dad's favorite," Max said. "Are they here yet?"

"Nope," Penelope said, glancing at the clock over the double oven. "I expect them any minute."

"Oh, sorry, hey, this is Ashley," Max said as the back door opened. "Ashley, this is Penelope."

Penelope wondered what Max's new girlfriend would look like. He normally preferred tall, dark-haired girls, but then again, she'd seen him date a lot of shorter blondes and redheads too.

"Hi," Penelope said. A young man stepped through the door and clapped Max on the shoulder. "You forgot these," he said, holding out a bag from Ferrara's, dinner rolls, from what they smelled like.

"Thanks, I'll take those," Penelope said, reaching for the bag.

"Thanks for including me," Ashley said, handing her the rolls. "Max goes on and on about your cooking."

Penelope blushed. "Oh, that's sweet of you. I was expecting..."

"Us to be earlier?" Max asked. "We had to hit the bakery. You know how it goes. Then traffic over the bridge from the city. There's a big parade today, maybe you heard about it?"

"Yeah," Penelope said with a laugh. "Actually, I was going to put it on in the library for the kids while I ice down some drinks."

"We're here to help," Ashley said. "Put me to work."

"Okay, well, there's some beer outside on the patio," Penelope said, nodding. "You can get it in the coolers for me and then grab the ice bags from the freezer in the garage."

"Done," Ashley said with a smile. His teeth were bright white next to his winter-tanned skin, and his blond good looks belonged in a fashion spread in a magazine. He propped two fingers at his brow and gave her a mock salute, then stepped toward the door. "I'm on the Red Carpet Catering crew today," he said before stepping outside.

Max watched him go and chuckled. "Where's Arlena?"

"They're getting dressed," Penelope said, eyeing the pastry boxes on the counter. "Who's your friend?"

"Oh, Ash," Max said. "I met him in that improv class I just took. He's auditioning, living in the city near me, just got called up for his first film. We've been hanging out. He's from out of town so I asked him over for Thanksgiving."

"Oh, cool," Penelope said. "I was expecting..."

"A lady friend like every year?" Max asked. He walked to the refrigerator and pulled open the door. "I'm taking a break from dating."

"Really?" Penelope asked, following him. She nudged him aside and pulled out a few blocks of cheese, some pâté, cured meats, and caviar she had placed on a platter. "That doesn't sound like the Max I know."

"It's not forever," Max said. "The holidays are a lot of pressure. And it's a weird time to start up a relationship. That's best for the new year. I'm tired of having ex-girlfriends in family photos taken at Christmas, you know?"

"Yeah, I know," Penelope said.

Max rubbed his hands together as he eyed the platter. "Charcuterie? Let me do this for you," he said.

"Are you sure?" Penelope asked.

"Of course," Max said. "If I know you, and I think I do, you've been up since dawn cooking for all of us. Let me do this easy bit."

"Okay, no excessive snacking," Penelope said, placing two French loaves on the kitchen island. "You can have some cheese but no dipping into the caviar until all the guests have arrived and had a chance at it. Company rule."

"I like it when you boss me around," Max said with a wriggle of his dark eyebrows.

"Stop," Penelope said.

The back door opened again and Randall Madison appeared in the kitchen.

"Happy Thanksgiving!" he bellowed.

"Daddy!" Arlena said, appearing from the hallway. She was dressed in skinny jeans and a bright red sweater, which set off her shiny black hair and olive skin perfectly.

Randall crushed his daughter in a hug, lifting her slightly off the ground like a big, leather-jacket wearing bear.

"Rand, can you take these?" Sybil Wilde stepped through the door, holding out two bottles of champagne.

"Of course, dear," Randall said, taking them from her and setting them on the counter. Once she was inside he helped her with her coat. "Where are the kids?"

"They're getting a soda from the guy outside," Sybil said, shaking out her hands. A smile spread across her face when she saw Arlena.

"Soda?" Penelope asked. When she had been catering the movie and was responsible for feeding the children, she knew soft drinks were on the definitely not list.

"Hello, Penelope," Sybil said with a laugh. She waved her manicured hand in the air breezily. "It's the holidays. Hello, my dear," Sybil said, grasping Arlena's hands and air kissing her on both cheeks.

"Hello, Sybil," Arlena said. "Happy Thanksgiving."

The door clattered open and Jackson and Dakota burst inside, holding their sodas in their hands. They wore matching sweaters, both brown with orange turkeys knitted on the front.

"Hey guys," Penelope said, stepping over to the kids. "You've grown a foot each since I've seen you."

"Not really a foot," Dakota said in a serious tone. "Some inches maybe."

"Don't correct Miss Penelope, sweetie," Sybil said.

Penelope winked at Sybil and knelt down to give them both a hug at the same time. "I'm so glad we're having Thanksgiving together," she whispered in their ears.

Jackson pulled away and focused on the bottle in his hand.

The door opened once more and Detective Joseph Baglioni, Penelope's boyfriend, stepped inside. Penelope looked up from her crouching position on the floor and smiled.

"Looks like the gang's all here," Joey said.

Although the kitchen was spacious, it was getting crowded.

"Why don't you all go to the library and watch the parade, and we'll have cocktails and appetizers in a little bit," Penelope said. The crowd slowly filed out of the room and headed for the back of the house where the large TV sat over the white marble fireplace. The whole room was done in white: white rugs, white sofas, white tables. She hoped no one had an accident and spilled caviar on Arlena's pristine furniture. But seeing how happy she was at that moment, Penelope guessed she wouldn't care.

When they'd all left except Max, who was busy assembling the meat and cheese board, Penelope grabbed Joey's hand and led him to the front foyer, out of sight of the kitchen.

"Happy Thanksgiving," Penelope whispered.

Joey looped his arms around her waist and pulled her into a hug. She breathed in the familiar scent of sandalwood.

"You look beautiful, and that turkey smells great," Joey said. He bent down and kissed her, which caused her stomach to do a little flip. "What did I do to deserve you?" he murmured in her ear.

Penelope laughed and hugged him tighter. "I don't know, but keep doing it."

Dakota skipped into the foyer and tugged on Joey's sleeve. He reluctantly pulled away from Penelope and looked down at the little girl.

"Are you a police officer?" Dakota asked.

Joey bent down and put his hands on his knees. "I sure am.

I'm a detective right here in New Jersey."

"We live in New Jersey too," Dakota said shyly. "Can I see your badge?"

"Dakota!" Sybil called from the other room.

Joey pulled his wallet from his back pocket and flipped it open, revealing his gold shield. He winked at Dakota, who squealed then tore off back to the library.

Joey stood back up and his expression turned serious. "How are you doing, really?"

"Oh," Penelope said. "I've been trying not to think about...everything that happened at the theater. I know that sounds selfish, but Thanksgiving is one of my favorite holidays."

"I know," Joey said. "It's not selfish. We all want to be festive regardless of what is happening in the world around us. That's normal."

"Or otherwise it would be too depressing," Penelope said. She crossed her arms tightly and shifted her weight. "But it's hard to think about her family ever enjoying the holiday again. They will always be reminded of her dying."

"Hey," Joey said. "Enough. I'm sorry I brought it up. I just wanted you to know, I called a friend of mine who works out of Manhattan North to see if there were updates."

"And were there any?" Penelope asked hesitantly.

"Yeah. Elspeth Connor was stabbed, but cause of death was strangulation. There were signs of sexual activity, too, but they're not sure if it was consensual or not."

Penelope put a hand over her mouth and stared at him. A bitter taste covered her tongue and she closed her eyes for a beat. "But it's possible she was sexually assaulted on top of everything else?"

"Or she was intimate with someone before she was attacked. Either one is possible."

"Her roommate is pretty adamant she wasn't seeing anyone," Penelope said. "I really hope she wasn't..." Penelope trailed off, not wanting to think about everything the poor girl had been through.

"Do they have any idea who might have done this?"

"No suspects yet," Joey said. "But I'm going to keep an ear out, especially with you working around that theater. I want you to promise me that you will be extra careful."

"I know," Penelope said. "I'm always careful."

Joey smiled and shook his head. "You're not, but I still love you."

Penelope rolled her eyes. "Who would think that kind of thing would happen in midtown, in the Theater District of all places in the city? It's tourist central, where people go to enjoy themselves."

"It's New York City, Penny," Joey said. "Bad things have a way of happening, no matter what neighborhood you're in."

CHAPTER 14

When it was time for dinner, Sam sat at one end of the table and Arlena at the other. Normally Randall was in the seat of honor, but Sam and Arlena had been serious for over two years now. Penelope loved seeing them so happy, even through their extended time apart when they were working on different projects. They were making it work. Penelope held Joey's hand under the table after they all got settled, and he leaned his head slightly over to touch hers.

Randall and Sybil sat across from them, flanked on either side by one of the kids. And Max and his friend Ashley sat next to Joey, rounding out the table.

"I'd like to wish you all, my family," Arlena's eyes landed on Ashley, who smiled widely in return, "old and new," she continued, "a very happy Thanksgiving. May the bounty of our table fill you with love and happiness."

Randall picked up his wine glass and said, "Cheers to that!"

"Very nicely put, sis," Max said, taking a sip of Sauvignon Blanc. "Especially the new friends part."

Sam stood and picked up the carving knife, then tugged the sleeves of his sweater back. Penelope had offered to carve the turkey in the kitchen after everyone had seen it, but Sam insisted on doing it at the table in front of everyone.

Penelope watched him, holding her breath slightly, as the knife and fork descended onto the bird. She exhaled when the first slice went smoothly and she could see the breast was plump and juicy. Sam's expression relaxed a bit too.

"Arlena and I are very happy you could all join us today," Sam said as he cut off another slice. He almost dropped the piece of turkey, but recovered and made it onto the platter. "We've been looking forward to having the family together for a while. And we'd like to invite you all," his eyes flicked to the newcomer next to Max, then he continued, "to a special holiday party we're hosting."

"Party?" Max asked.

"We'd like to celebrate with you all," Arlena said. "Sam thought it would be nice if we had a formal gathering, all of us together."

"How much turkey can I have?" Jackson asked. Sybil shushed him and smiled at Sam to continue.

"Yes, a Christmas party," Sam said. He sliced another piece of turkey, then inched over to focus on a leg. He was getting the hang of the carving, Penelope noticed, and sliced into a thigh with more confidence. "A celebration."

"Sounds good, Sam," Randall said. "When's this soiree happening?"

"On the twenty-third," Sam said. "Two days before Christmas. I promise, you're not going to want to miss it."

Sam bent over and looked into the bird's cavity. "What's this?" he asked, a look of confusion on his face.

Penelope's heart picked up a beat as she watched him. Did she forget to remove the gizzards? No, impossible. She'd used them to make the gravy. Her legs tensed and she thought about standing up.

"That's weird," Sam said, bending down further.

"What's in there?" Dakota asked, craning her neck to see.

"Now, how did this get here?" Sam asked.

"What?" several people asked at once.

Sam stood up and held a small box in the air. The distinctive teal blue hue told everyone exactly where it had come from.

"Sam," Arlena said, her voice quavering, her eyes jumping from his face to the box. "What are you up to?"

Sam smiled widely, set down the carving knife and walked to

the other end of the table. Max pulled out his phone and began recording. Randall stared, his mouth slightly open, in complete surprise.

Sam got down on one knee, gracefully, as if he'd practiced it many times before. "Arlena Sofia Madison, will you marry me?"

CHAPTER 15

"Yes!" Arlena cried, then clapped both hands over her mouth. Her eyes grew even wider as she looked at the blue box in Sam's palm. He opened the it slowly and Arlena's gaze drifted from his eyes to the large diamond ring inside.

"Oh, Sam, it's beautiful," Arlena said. She slipped the ring on her finger and threw her arms around his neck.

Randall began to clap as Sam and Arlena stood and embraced next to her chair. "Congratulations, you two," he said. He took Sybil's hand in his and gave it a squeeze. She smiled at him in return.

"That was some surprise, Sam," Joey said appreciatively. He put his arm around Penelope's shoulders and hugged her close. Dakota giggled and Jackson rolled his eyes, then looked longingly at the turkey.

Arlena finally let go of Sam and he set the box on the table next to her plate. Arlena shot a glance at Penelope, then looked down at her hand, tilting it from side to side to admire the square cut gem.

"It's so perfect, Sam," Arlena said.

"So, the party I was talking about before," Sam said, "is actually our engagement party. Luckily Arlena said yes, so I won't lose the deposit I put on the place." A few chuckles went around the table.

"Daddy?" Arlena asked.

Randall stood up from his chair and shook hands with Sam. "I had no idea you were going to do it today, during Thanksgiving dinner."

"You knew what he was up to?" Arlena asked, taking her seat and eyeing her ring again.

"Sam very kindly called and asked for my blessing. But that was over a month ago," Randall said. "Well played, young man."

"You might tell them our news too," Sybil said, "since we're all celebrating."

"News?" Penelope asked.

"Sybil and I are getting married too," Randall said, nodding. He sat back down and held her hand again. Jackson sighed and crossed his arms at his chest, still staring at the bird in the center of the table.

"What?" Arlena asked, her smile faltering. "When?"

"Tomorrow," Randall said.

"Dad," Max said, "what are you talking about? What do you mean you're getting married tomorrow?"

"Well, maybe not tomorrow," Randall said, eyeing Sybil next to him. "But as soon as possible."

Arlena and Max stared at each other a beat, then Sam said, "This calls for a toast! It's not every day two Madisons get engaged, right?"

"Well, in Dad's case..." Max began.

Penelope cleared her throat and leveled her gaze at Max.

"Good one, son," Randall said. "But this time, I've met my match."

Arlena's smile amped back to full brightness as Sam made his way back to the turkey and started filling the platter again. Jackson looked relived.

"I'll get the champagne," Penelope said. "Double congratulations are in order." She inched her chair back and hurried to the kitchen.

Penelope paused at the island and placed her hand on the cool granite, steadying herself for a moment. A wave of emotion came over her, one of pure happiness for Arlena. A major shift was about to take place, one that would impact her life too. Her heartbeat settled and she smiled, then took a deep breath and straightened her shoulders.

"Is the bathroom through here?" Ashley appeared in the doorway, causing Penelope to jump a little.

"Oh, yeah," she said, "there's a powder room in the hallway." She pointed toward the foyer.

"This is a very different kind of Thanksgiving than I'm used to," Ashley said, shaking his head. "Talk about feeling like a third wheel."

"You shouldn't feel like that, Ashley," Penelope said with a smile. "The Madisons are very inviting."

"Yeah," Ashley said. "When I told Max I was going to get some takeout and watch football, he insisted I come with him to dinner."

Penelope opened the refrigerator and pulled out the champagne. "That sounds like Max." A muffled burst of laughter floated to them from the other room.

"Can I help with that?" Ashley asked.

"Sure," Penelope said, placing the bottles on the counter. She went to the cupboard above the wine rack and reached up for the champagne flutes. When she turned back around she caught a second of Ashley staring at her. He quickly ducked his head and focused on peeling the foil from the first bottle.

"Thanks," Penelope said after he got the first one done. "Let's leave the second until we see how this one goes down. Bathroom's right through there." She nodded toward the hallway and watched him go.

Penelope hooked six flutes upside down in her fingers and went back to the dining room.

CHAPTER 16

After Max had helped Penelope clean up after dinner and then joined his friend in the library to either talk or watch football, Penelope slid up on one of the stools and swiped open her iPad. Randall, Sybil, Arlena, and Sam were still in the dining room, lingering over pie and coffee. The kids were in the library too, sitting on bean bag chairs Sybil had brought for them and playing video games on their iPads.

A thought came to her and she Googled the name Richard Sotheby, adding the words "Manhattan" and "murder." One result came up, a short piece in the *New York Times*. She read through it quickly.

"What are you doing in here by yourself, Penny?" Joey called from the doorway. "Wanna come watch some football?"

"I'll be there in a little bit," Penelope said with a smile. "Just having a quiet moment, decompressing after dinner service." She picked up the stemless wine glass in front of her and took a sip of red. Joey came over and hugged her from behind, glancing at the tablet on the counter. "What are you reading?"

"It's an article about Mrs. Sotheby's husband. He was shot and killed back in the seventies, when they were first married."

"Yeah, I remember her saying something about that once," Joey said. He sat down next to Penelope and picked up the iPad. "They never caught the guy who did it, if I remember correctly."

"Yeah, that's right," Penelope said. "I checked in on her yesterday, brought her some tea when I was in the city."

"How is she doing?"

"Good," Penelope said. "They are happy."

"Hey," Joey said. "Are you okay?"

"Yeah," Penelope said. "It's just, I'm not going to see my folks for the holidays this year. I think it's making me a little sad."

"You want to go visit them soon? I'll take a look at some flights."

"Maybe in the spring," Penelope said. "They're taking a cruise over Christmas."

Joey rubbed her shoulder and she put her head in her hand.

"That's something about Arlena and Sam, huh?" Joey asked.

"Sure is. I had no idea."

"It's good timing, you ask me," Joey said, brushing a loose strand of hair behind her ear. She leaned into his touch, the familiar feel of his rough finger on her cheek.

"Why's that?" Penelope asked.

"Well, when we find the perfect house, you know, it won't be as hard for you to move," Joey said. "They're going to be all into each other, starting a family probably."

"Yeah," Penelope whispered. She bit the inside of her cheek. "I didn't say it was going to be hard."

"Hey, what's the matter?" Joey asked. "You upset you're the only girl at the table who didn't get a ring at Thanksgiving?"

Penelope laughed quietly. "No," she said, "it's not that at all. I'm happy with you and me, us, how we are. Totally. It's just...I don't know."

"What? You know you can tell me," Joey said, brushing her cheek again.

"Change is hard," Penelope said. "I know it has to happen, but I think of Arlena as family, and this is my home. I haven't even told her yet about us thinking of moving in together."

"You haven't mentioned it?" Joey asked.

"I don't know, it hasn't ever seemed like the right time," Penelope said, avoiding his gaze.

"Are you sure you still want to move in with me?" Joey asked.

Penelope hesitated. "I think so. Yes."

"You sound like you're having second thoughts," Joey said, deflating.

Penelope grabbed his hand and held it tight. "I'm not having second thoughts about us, Joey. I just get a little panicky thinking about the future and the uncertainty ahead."

"You can always count on me, Penny," Joey said. "I won't let you down."

"I don't think anyone goes into a marriage or takes big steps in a relationship thinking things aren't going to go well. And yet people split up every day."

"If you want to take more time to think about it..." Joey said half-heartedly.

"No," Penelope said with another squeeze of his hand. "I believe in us."

"Well, like I said, no time like the present, then, to let Arlena know," Joey said. "The metaphorical present, I mean. Not right now."

"But what if me moving out changes everything between me and Arlena? What if we drift apart?"

"Aw come on," Joey said, pulling her into a hug. "You guys are always going to be close. You're best friends. Everything that's happening is good. Growing up and leaving the nest will be rough, but I'll be there to help you."

Penelope laughed. "Don't tease me," she said. "My parents moved away when I was in culinary school, sold the house I grew up in. I felt like I was all on my own and I wasn't really ready for it."

Joey tipped her chin up with his finger and looked her in the eyes. "You're not going to be alone, or feel that way ever again. Trust me, Penny Blue."

He kissed her lightly on the lips and she brushed her worries to the side, if only for a moment.

CHAPTER 17

Joey was up with Penelope before dawn. They crept down the steps and Penelope kissed him goodbye at the kitchen door. Randall, his fiancée and his soon-to-be young stepchildren had gone home after the football game, and Max and his friend Ashley had headed back to Manhattan a little bit after them. Joey had stayed with her, hugging her until she drifted off to sleep.

"Have a good day," Joey said. "Be careful in the city today, okay? Keep your eyes open."

"Of course," Penelope said with a smile. "I'll be careful. You too."

After he'd gone, Penelope made a cup of coffee and scanned the news on her iPad. After a quick search she opened an updated article about Elspeth's murder. Penelope blew at the steam rising from her coffee as she enlarged a group of thumbnail photos. One was of Elspeth, probably her professional headshot, all smiles with a tumble of red hair falling around her shoulders. Her cheeks were rosy and her eyes bright green, the color of an Irish field.

The next photo was of an older couple, the caption beneath identifying them as Gerald and Florence Connor, Elspeth's parents. The article said they had arrived in New York from Seattle the previous afternoon. Florence wore large black sunglasses that obscured most of her face. Penelope drew her eyes to the woman's tense jaw and her mouth, which was slightly open and spoke of the pain and worry the woman must be feeling. Elspeth's father was a large, round man with a shiny bald head and a scarf tied tightly around his neck. Unlike his wife, Gerald Connor's face conveyed anger. Penelope stared at him a for a few moments. He reminded her of someone, but she couldn't place it immediately, like an old movie star from the forties.

The article went on to say they'd come to assist the police in finding out who had killed their daughter, a young dancer with lots of promise who had landed one of the best jobs in her field: a spot with the Big Apple Dancers.

Penelope took a sip of her coffee and slid her finger across the screen, opening up the entertainment section. There was another article that mentioned Elspeth, but this one focused more on the history of the theater itself and the upcoming Christmas Extravaganza. The theater had changed hands several times through the years and almost gone bankrupt more than once before being saved by the current group of owners, collectively known as the Beckwith Group. And now Randall had injected a bit of money as well, which when Armand had talked about it, sounded like it was needed to keep them afloat once more.

"You're up early," Arlena said in a low voice as she entered the kitchen.

"I could say the same about you," Penelope said. "How does your first morning as an engaged woman feel?"

Arlena smiled sleepily, her hand drifting up slowly to admire her ring once again. "Wonderful."

She shuffled to the counter and pulled down a mug to make her morning tea.

"I'm so happy for you guys," Penelope said.

"I know you are," Arlena said. She set her mug of hot water on the island and hugged Penelope before taking the seat next to her.

"Can you believe Daddy?" Arlena said with a laugh.

"Yeah," Penelope laughed. "He's a romantic."

"We talked at the table last night," Arlena said, rolling her eyes. "We agreed me and Sam will make our engagement announcement first, and then Daddy and Sybil can do their thing." She waved her hand in the air dismissively. "This is my one and only marriage. This will be his fifth, Sybil's second."

"So, you get to go first? That's fair," Penelope asked.

"I don't care who goes first, I just want his full attention for my wedding. I want him to walk me down the aisle. I didn't get to have my dad with me growing up, but I definitely want him with me now."

"How about your mom?" Penelope asked. "Will things be awkward with them?"

"I don't think so," Arlena said. "She moved on a long time ago. She loves living out in the country in her cabin, painting, hanging out with her friends. She's got a boyfriend now too, for like ten years now."

"Why doesn't she ever come down during the holidays?" Penelope asked, then paused, wondering if she'd overstepped.

"Mom...let's just say, she's not welcome in the US," Arlena said. "She was quite the activist back in the day, she might have a record. I'm not sure of all the details, but there are outstanding charges against her and a few others, some kind of protest where they tied themselves to trees, and when the police came to break it up, an officer was killed. Not by any of the protestors, he fell from a tall tree, but they were all charged in the death."

"Oh wow," Penelope said. "I had no idea."

"Yeah," Arlena said. "She's much more comfortable in Canada. I should try to get up there again soon to see her."

Penelope got up to refresh her coffee and Arlena picked up her iPad.

"I guess we have to get back into work mode here soon," Arlena said. "You still up for seeing the show tonight, help me make some notes?"

"Yes," Penelope said as she fiddled with the coffee machine. "I'm up for it. I also need to get a sense from you what we'll need meal wise. I've never catered a documentary before, so I'm learning on this one."

Arlena flipped through a few articles on the news site Penelope had been reading as she spoke.

"There will be twenty of us on site with camera, sound, and

lighting people," Arlena said. "And then we have an office across the street for the editing suite. Daddy said last night we should preview dailies each night, so we know what we've got, and can reshoot any footage we may have missed, or didn't come out well the next day."

"I guess that's better than waiting until the end and realizing you didn't get something on film," Penelope said, watching her mug fill.

"Right. Because once it's over, it's over..." Arlena trailed off. "What the...?"

"What is it?" Penelope asked.

"Entertainment page," Arlena said, her voice picking up speed. "A double engagement for the Madison acting clan. Arlena and Randall Madison announce their impending nuptials on the same day. The family that acts together weds together..." Arlena balled her hand into a fist.

"How do they have that?" Penelope asked.

Arlena banged her fist on the counter. "Damn! This is exactly what I meant. The story is already about both of us, all four of us."

"But how do they know already?" Penelope asked again.

Arlena blew out a sigh. "It has to be that Ashley guy. Max's friend. He probably got paid to give them the scoop."

Penelope came back around and read through the blurb. "The time stamp on the blog entry is last night," she murmured.

"That little creep," Arlena seethed.

"So, what now?" Penelope asked. "Send a correction, or ask them to take it down?"

"No," Arlena said, shaking her head. "Sometimes that brings more attention to something than it ever would've gotten otherwise."

"Hey babe," Sam said groggily from the hallway. He shuffled into the kitchen and kissed her on the head. "Morning, Pen."

Penelope smiled and gave him a concerned glance then drew her eyes back to the iPad.

"What's up?" he asked, looking at the article. "Hey! The news is out already?"

"No," Arlena said tightly. "Not the way I want it to be."

"Hey, it's okay," Sam said, rubbing her shoulders. "I'm ready for the world to know I'm marrying the perfect woman."

Arlena blushed and smiled. "I do too, babe. I just want to control our story," Arlena said.

"I can call my publicist," Sam said, letting her go and heading over to the coffee maker. "They can send out a release, word it how you want."

Arlena sighed. "You mean the publicity department at the movie studio?"

"Yeah," Sam shrugged. "That's their job."

"For your movies," Arlena said. "I think we need a personal publicist. Here on the east coast."

"Okay," Sam said over his shoulder. "Whatever you want to do."

Arlena crossed her arms and sat back against the stool.

"I'm going to get cleaned up," Penelope said, picking up her mug and heading toward the hallway. "Can we meet in an hour about the production? I want to get my vendors lined up for the first day of filming."

"Saturday, right," Arlena said distractedly. "I need to make a list. Call Daddy about the Big Apple documentary, get myself organized to begin work on this project, hire a publicist and a wedding planner and..."

Penelope paused, waiting for her to finish.

"...kill my brother."

Chapter 18

Randall sat at the dining room table a few hours later. Penelope set a plate of cheese and fruit in the center of the table and tall glasses of lemon water at the three spots.

"Thanks, Pen," Randall said. He lightly grasped her wrist in his strong hand and held her in place for another moment. "Arlena is going to be calling on you with the wedding. I want you to know we really appreciate you helping out on this project."

Penelope smiled and leaned down to hug him. "I know you do. And I wouldn't dream of not helping."

"Okay, that's done," Arlena said as she stepped into the dining room from the hall, ending a call and setting her phone on the table. "I have three wedding planners lined up to give presentations."

"Presentations?" Randall asked.

"You know," Arlena said quickly, "they're going to pitch me on their best ideas for a Madison-Cavanaugh wedding."

Randall chuckled. "That's great, sweetheart."

"Daddy," Arlena said reproachfully. "This is how it's done."

"Arlena," Randall said with a smile, "I of all people know how weddings are done. This will be my fifth, remember?"

Arlena rolled her eyes and sighed. "I know, Daddy."

Penelope cleared her throat. "So, what have you brought for us today?" She glanced at the thick folder in front of Randall on the table.

"Glad you asked," Randall said with a smile. "This is my mother's, your grandmother's," he flicked his eyes to Arlena across the table, "personal papers, diaries, and photos—her archive during the time she was a dancer in the city. I'm picturing this as our backdrop, source material for the doc."

Randall flipped open the folder and slid a few photos across the lacquered wood toward Arlena.

"She was beautiful," Penelope murmured, glancing at a photo. The dancers wore elaborate headpieces in the shape of Christmas trees, with ornaments hanging down, shimmering in the stage lights. The black and white photo caused their painted lips to look black, but Penelope imagined they were a deep red to match what she guessed were red and green bodysuit leotards.

"That headgear was heavy," Randall said. "Almost five pounds. My mom talked about her aching neck, sore legs, and blistered feet."

"They look so elegant," Arlena said, flipping to another photo.

"That's showbiz," Randall said darkly.

"So, the focus of the documentary, the subject really, is Grandma Ruby?"

"No," Randall said. His fingers brushed the leather-bound book that sat on more documents in the file. "She's the focus of the piece. The subject as I envision it is the life of the dancers themselves, from the beginning of the production to now: how these girls get to be Big Apple Dancers, what they go through mentally and physically and how that has changed over time."

Arlena jotted a few notes. "Okay, who do we want for director?" Arlena asked, her pen hovering over the pad.

"I want you to be the director," Randall said.

Arlena's lips curled into a smile. "Really? You said co-producer when we first started talking about this last year. I thought you wanted to hire a friend to direct, an unbiased eye, you said."

Randall set his palms on the table on either side of the papers in front of him. "I've been thinking about that, and you're the perfect, most logical choice. We know our family better than anyone, and you can get to the real story."

"Everyone is talking about how we need more women in

charge," Penelope chimed in.

Arlena bit her bottom lip and nodded. "You'll be there to help me, though, right, Daddy? I've never directed before."

"Absolutely," Randall said. "And Max, too."

Arlena rolled her eyes. "I know he's never directed anything. Except a torpedo at my private life."

"What are you talking about?" Randall asked.

"You didn't see the news yesterday? Somehow the press got wind of my engagement," Arlena said. "And yours," she added in a mumble. "Obviously someone blabbed, and the only person who could've done it is Max, or his friend Ashley."

"So what? I don't pay attention those gossip rags," Randall said. "And you shouldn't either. It will drive you crazy. Focus on your work."

"You don't care what people are saying about you publicly?" Penelope asked.

"I stopped reading reviews of my movies, and giving attention to reporters over twenty years ago," Randall said. "Even good reviews or news can distract you from what you really should be doing...giving your best performance and focusing on the job at hand."

"It was easier to ignore things when it was just a few magazines and newspapers," Arlena said. "Now literally everyone is a critic. Or reporter."

"All the more reason to tune that stuff out," Randall said. "I just think if you take all of that in, good and bad comments, it's going to change the way you act...I don't want to be reacting to public opinion all the time. Trust me, tune it out. And don't be mad at your brother. It's not the worst thing in the world to give a friend a place to go on Thanksgiving."

"And spoiler alert the most important news I've had in my life?" Arlena said testily. "Unless it was Sybil who spilled the beans and you're too afraid to tell me."

Randall showed her his palms and chuckled. "I swear, it wasn't her. You can leave us out of it."

Arlena drummed her fingers on the wooden table and leveled her gaze at Randall. He put his hands behind his head and leaned back, smiling at his daughter.

"Do we know what crew members we'll need then?" Penelope said, veering the conversation back to work. Maybe Randall had a point. Arlena should focus on the things she could control and let go of the rest.

"Yes," Randall said, plucking a sample call sheet from the stack of papers. "Here are the positions that will need to be filled. As director and co-producer, you can choose who you want to fill them."

"I suggest we keep the crew on the small side, for financial reasons since we're footing the bill," Randall said. "Plus, I think working with a smaller team will give the film a more intimate feel."

"That makes sense," Arlena said, jotting a few notes.

"And our working space in the penthouse can only hold so many bodies comfortably, once you get the editorial suite set up," Randall said.

"Is it the same building the theater uses?" Penelope asked. "Where the dancers live?"

"Yep. The penthouse has a kitchen, too," Randall said. "And you can use the alley for your catering trucks."

Penelope wrote the word "alley" on her notepad, and the image of Elspeth lying on the pavement flashed in front of her eyes. Everything at the theater was moving on without her, even in the spot where she was found dead.

Arlena's phone pinged on the table next to her and she glanced at the screen. "Looks like we're getting somewhere now."

"We are," Randall said. "And I'd suggest you review some of these things too, familiarize yourself with Grandma Ruby, some of the history of the place."

"Of course," Arlena said. Her phone pinged again. "Will we see you at rehearsal later, Daddy?"

"I'll be there," Randall said.

Arlena stood up and left the room, pulling the phone to her ear on the way out.

"She might need an assistant," Randall murmured. "She can't rely on you for everything, you know."

Penelope laughed. "You know, that's actually not a bad idea." She picked up one of the photos from the table. "This was Ruby?" A woman stood on a city sidewalk in front of a storefront, a stole wrapped around her shoulders and a cigarette clutched between two fingers of her gloved hand.

"The one and only," Randall said with a small smile.

"What was she like?" Penelope asked, staring at the woman's face in the photograph.

"I don't remember a lot, only that she was always in a hurry, bouncing off the walls. She was a ball of energy. My aunt called her a live wire, which I didn't understand as a kid."

"Are there any pictures of Ruby and your father?" Penelope asked.

"None that I've seen," Randall said. "They weren't married. To each other, at least."

Arlena's voice drifted in from the other room. They could hear she was talking about wedding plans, and a time for one of the planners to give a presentation.

"I don't remember him," Randall continued. "He was a Marine, died in Okinawa during the war. Ruby was pregnant."

"That's so sad," Penelope said. She set the photo down and picked up another one. Ruby was older in this one, and wearing a western costume, with a long skirt and a lace shawl around her shoulders.

"She was in *Oklahoma!* in that picture," Randall said. "1947. The next year she appeared in the holiday show at the Vitrine, and she did that for four more years until..."

Randall's normally confident expression was replaced by a faraway look, an emptiness in his eyes.

"What happened to her, if you don't mind my asking?"

Randall shook his head and "My aunt who I went to live with said my mom's heart was too big, and it got broken too many times," Randall said. "I didn't know what she meant."

"Sounds like things were rough for you growing up," Penelope said.

"Not really," Randall said. "Aunt Tula was fun, but she also didn't take any nonsense from us kids. Tula took us to the theater, and to the movies every Friday after school. I grew up with my cousins, who were like a brother and sister to me. My uncle worked at one of the big record labels at the time, so I met musicians and could get tickets to any shows I wanted. I was very lucky I got to be one of their kids, in the end."

"When did you decide to be an actor?" Penelope asked.

"In my teens," Randall said, rubbing his chin. "Me and Tula still had our Friday night movie routine and we saw *The Great Escape* near Times Square. I walked out of that theater knowing I wanted to be just like Steve McQueen one day. A month later, Tula had signed me up for acting classes. She took me to my first audition, too. The rest..." he spread his arms wide, the confidence returning to his face, "is history."

"That's a great story," Penelope said.

"Tula showed me a lot of things," Randall said. "But the most important was how to love, and to follow your dreams."

CHAPTER 19

Armand met Penelope and Arlena at the front door of the theater, then led them down the main aisle toward the stage.

"Big night tonight," Armand said, excitement flitting through his words. "The girls have already been through the numbers three times. They're on break now."

"Armand! We need to finish this before they come back to stage," someone yelled from the orchestra pit. He waved at the conductor who was holding up some papers.

"Please, make yourselves at home," Armand said graciously. "Much to attend to at the moment, but I'll join you later to watch the final dress rehearsal."

"Thank you, Armand," Arlena said, sliding one of her gloves off. "Don't let us keep you."

"Oh, how stupid of me," Armand said, glancing at their coats. "I forgot to take your coats in the front."

"I've got it," Penelope said. She slipped off her short wool pea coat and took Arlena's long white one from her. "I'll go hang them up."

"Don't worry, the front door is locked," Armand said. "Your things will be safe this time."

Armand hurried toward the orchestra pit, waving his hands in the air over his head when the conductor began speaking to him again.

"I'm going to slip backstage, talk to a few of the performers," Arlena said. "Scope out who might have the most interesting stories."

"Okay, I'll figure out where my team can set up," Penelope said with a nod.

"Oh," Arlena said, reaching into her purse. "Here's the key to the office across the street. Seventeenth floor, Suite A. I spent the afternoon making calls and putting together the team, and they'll be here tomorrow."

"Got it," Penelope said. "You want to hang on to your purse?"

"Um," Arlena said. "Yeah, I'm going to ask Armand for a locker in the dressing room for our valuables."

"Good idea," Penelope said.

Arlena went backstage toward the dressing rooms and Penelope took their coats out to the lobby.

The key was in the lock of the old door, the same tarnished brass color of all the other metal in the room. She swung the door open and stepped inside, flipping on the light switch right inside the door. Stepping to the back wall, Penelope hung up the coats, the empty metal hangers rattling against each other. The door clicked closed behind her and she jerked her head around, the feeling of another presence in the small space suddenly making her feel claustrophobic.

Even though she thought she heard the sound of someone breathing right behind her, she was alone in the small space. She could hear the orchestra warming up, the sound of the music muffled by the thick walls of the coat closet. Yellow light from the bulb above threw triangles of shadows across the thin carpet beneath her feet.

Penelope sighed and went to the door. She turned the knob, but it just spun in her hand. She tried twisting it the other way, but it was no use. She was locked inside the coat closet.

"I can't believe this," Penelope said, thinking about the key in the lock on the other side of the door. She knocked on the top half of the door. "Hello? Anyone out there?"

The music from the theater got louder as the orchestra began rehearsing a song.

"Hey!" Penelope called loudly. She slapped her hand on the

wood and listened to it rattle.

The light above her flipped off suddenly, plunging her into darkness.

"Come on," Penelope said. She reached out toward the wall where she remembered the light switch was. "Leave it to me to lock myself in a coat closet on the first day of work."

The wall beneath her hand seemed to vibrate, and she felt a small electrical shock.

Penelope pulled her hand back and took a few steps back from the door. Shaking out her hand, she dug in her messenger bag and pulled out her phone, pressing the flashlight button.

Confirming she was indeed locked inside the closet, she dialed Arlena's number.

"You're where?" Arlena said with a chuckle.

"You heard me," Penelope said. "Can you come rescue me?"

"Be right there," Arlena said. "I say we avoid the closet from now on."

"Good idea," Penelope said.

Arlena hung up and Penelope pointed her phone around the small space, illuminating the walls and carpet on the floor. Something glinted in the light, in the far back corner. Penelope picked it up, thinking someone had lost an earring.

She held the small piece of gold in front of her phone, turning it from side to side to see it better. It was a small round token with a picture of a dragon etched on the back. She stared at it for a second then turned it over in her hand. The back had been inscribed but the metal was worn and several of the words had been rubbed away.

The door rattled open and Arlena stood on the other side.

"What happened?" she asked.

"I don't know," Penelope said. "I think this closet is possessed."

CHAPTER 20

After Arlena rescued her from the self-locking coat closet with the timed light switch that was set to turn off after one minute, Penelope joined her in the dressing room to meet some of the Big Apple Dancers.

"Thanks for coming to my rescue," Penelope said.

"Anytime," Arlena said with a chuckle. "I feel so brave."

"I was really trapped," Penelope said grimly. "I freaked out a little in the dark."

"Anyone would," Arlena said, looking up into the rafters. The rigging above the stage where several lights and cables hung, loomed like giant spiders in a web. "If you ask me, all old buildings in the city are a little mysterious."

One of the dancers sat in a chair, her foot pulled up in her lap so she could massage her toes with her hands.

"Did Bainbridge lock you in the closet?" the woman asked. Her eyes were rimmed with black eyeliner, her hair pulled tightly into a bun at the back of her head. She had on a sports bra and leggings, her muscular body twisted like a pretzel in the chair.

"Excuse me?" Penelope asked. "Who is Bainbridge?"

"The Vitrine Theater ghost," the dancer said.

Arlena turned and looked at Penelope, then back at the girl. "We've never heard of a ghost here at the theater."

The dancer rolled her eyes and sighed. "He's a legend around here. Victor Bainbridge was lead actor here in like, 1900, I think. He fell from the apartment upstairs, down through all the rigging and scaffolds, hanging himself accidentally during a performance.

They say he haunts the theater now."

"Oh my," Penelope said. "Well, I was a little creeped out, but I don't believe in ghosts."

The dancer stood up from her chair and shrugged, shaking out her gracefully long limbs. "I do."

After the girl left, Arlena laughed. "There you have it. I've rescued you from a haunted closet."

"Let's get back to work," Penelope said. "I prefer things that I know are real."

CHAPTER 21

The changing rooms the dancers used were six sectioned off areas with heavy red curtains they could pull across a rod in the front. A tall blonde performer in a dark blue leotard stood outside of one, texting on her phone. She lifted her eyes for a second and gave Arlena a smile, then looked back down at the screen.

"I'm going to hang out here, talk to a couple of the ladies," Arlena said.

Penelope continued down the hall, looking for the kitchen area. There were windows at the back of the theater that lit the space in a hazy warmth.

Penelope caught pieces of different conversations behind the curtains as she passed. When she reached the final one, the curtain opened, and Penelope came face to face with one from the troupe, her face heavy with makeup. The changing room behind her was strewn with clothes, four tall narrow lockers and two makeup tables with soft lights glowing all the way around the edges.

"Hey, sorry," Penelope said. "Is it this way to the break room?"

"Yes, just through there," the woman said. Penelope was mesmerized by the thick coating of lipstick on her mouth. "Just around the corner. You can't miss it."

"Thanks," Penelope said.

"No problem," the dancer said. She was in her stage costume, and the silver sequins shimmered in the light.

"You look beautiful," Penelope said.

The dancer cocked her hip and gave Penelope a wink. "Much obliged."

Penelope followed the hallway to the end, turning right and going through another door.

She entered a small kitchen complete with a tiny stove that looked like it hadn't been used in years, a few dusty looking cabinets and a sink full of coffee cups. She opened the refrigerator and saw a few sodas and some cupcakes wrapped in plastic, and a half-empty jar of olives.

Penelope put her hands on her hips and turned around, staring at the small space, picturing where she might set things up.

Heading back out to the dressing rooms, Penelope came across another dancer, the one who had been stretching on the floor.

"Hey, do they have coffee set up anywhere? Like a craft service table?"

"Once in a while they bring in sandwiches from the deli," the dancer said. "We're basically on our own for anything else."

"Not this year," Penelope said. "You guys will have to tell me what you like. I'll be sure to have it all."

She continued on, looking for Arlena, finally stepping back through onto the stage. Music was playing and five of the dancers were going through one of the routines dressed in matching sparkly leotards.

Arlena and Armand were standing near the front row in the aisle, watching the dancers as they chatted to each other. Martha eyed the women sharply, tapping a forefinger on her bicep in time with the music.

Penelope descended the steps and joined Armand and Arlena.

"Okay, two minutes," Martha shouted and clapped her hands. "Take your places."

"Let's watch," Armand said, motioning to an aisle a few rows back from the front.

Martha stood stage center as the dancers moved into place, forming an inverted V on the stage. A dancer hurried out from backstage and took the empty spot at the top point of the V, her costume slightly different than the others, and she had a headpiece in the shape of a star on her head.

"Meredith is this year's Snow Queen," Armand mumbled as the woman got into position.

"How do you choose the queen?" Arlena asked.

Armand crossed his legs in a smooth motion. "The queen chooses herself, really. It's that one dancer each year that has that special...how do you say it? Star quality. Martha and I have always agreed on who to pick, actually."

"And she's the queen for the whole season?" Penelope asked.

"Generally," Armand said, "unless she can't manage the demands. It's an honor these dancers work hard for, so they don't easily give it up."

The orchestra settled as the conductor stood, raising his baton and flicking his wrist. The music began and the dancers stood frozen, each looking slightly to the left, their legs perfectly posed and identical to one another.

The lines of dancers began to move, marching in place in unison until the V became a straight line. Then they split into four groups, turning in circles together that looked like snowflakes rotating on the stage.

Martha watched from the front row, her head slightly bobbing along with the music.

A loud clatter from the lobby jarred Penelope from her rapt attention to the production on the stage.

"Why isn't that door locked again?" Armand said, turning his head. "For the life of me I can't understand—"

"Where is she?" someone shouted from the lobby.

A man burst through the curtains and rushed down the aisle toward the stage.

It was Elspeth's father. Penelope recognized him from the picture in the article she'd read.

"Where is she?" he bellowed. Spotting Martha in the front row, he charged toward her. Martha turned her head in annoyance, and her expression remained one of stern disapproval as Mr. Connor got closer.

Detective Doyle lumbered down the aisle after Mr. Connor,

with Mrs. Connor close behind.

"You tell me right now what happened to my daughter," Mr. Connor said. "Lord knows what's happened to her in this godforsaken place."

"Stop now," Martha yelled at the stage, and the dancers froze in place. Martha eyed Mr. Connor warily.

"What is the meaning of this?" Armand said, standing up from his seat. Arlena and Penelope watched him hurry behind Mrs. Connor and join them all in the front with Martha.

"Mr. Connor," Martha said. "What seems to be the problem?"

"The problem?" Mr. Connor almost spit. "Where is she?"

"I'm sorry," Armand said. "I know you've had an awful shock. But I don't think it's a good idea for you to see where she was found. Try to remember her as she was, full of life, and beautiful."

Mrs. Connor's shoulders caved and she held a handkerchief up to her lips.

"You tell me right now," Mr. Connor said, his rage boiling just beneath the surface. "Where is my daughter?"

"What do you mean? She is with the police, at the morgue," Martha said, dropping her voice on the last word and looking away from him.

"Whoever that girl is in the morgue," Mr. Connor said loudly, "is not Elspeth Connor."

CHAPTER 22

A flurry of gasps sounded from the stage. The dancers and musicians stared at the Connors uneasily.

"What are you talking about?" Martha asked. "Of course it's Elspeth."

"That girl we saw is not our daughter," Mrs. Connor said meekly.

"Well, who is it then, Detective?" Armand asked.

Detective Doyle shook his head. "They're saying they can't positively identify her. I tend to believe them, based on the family photos they brought with them from Seattle."

"Tell them about the contacts," Mr. Connor said, his voice cutting through the air like a knife.

Doyle crossed his arms tightly, the shoulders of his coat rising a few inches to reach his ears. "It appears our murder victim had her hair dyed red and was wearing emerald green contacts. She's really a brunette with brown eyes."

"What is going on?" Penelope whispered to Arlena, who shrugged in response.

"I assure you," Armand said, "the same person who was in our rehearsals is the same person who auditioned and won a spot in our troupe."

"You're absolutely sure?" Doyle asked. "You're willing to swear to that?"

Armand nodded his head, but a look of uncertainty had settled on his face.

"It's just that..." Martha said cautiously, "we auditioned over three hundred dancers...it's possible to confuse one with another, Armand, isn't it? When we meet them for three minutes at a time, most of them unknown to us?"

Armand shrugged his shoulders and rubbed his hands together. "Well, putting it that way, I guess anything is possible."

"How many faces can you really remember out of all of them?" Martha continued. "Sometimes I'm just looking at their legs, to make sure they'll match up on the kick line, if they're strong enough to hold the line all season."

Armand pinched the bridge of his nose and closed his eyes. "Martha as always is very wise. But from what we knew, she was Elspeth Connor, at least the past few weeks during rehearsal."

"If anyone here has any information about the identity of the woman found in the alley, we are asking you to come forward now," Detective Doyle said.

Several of the dancers shook their heads. A couple of them had tears in their eyes.

"Now I want you all to think back," Doyle urged them. "Did at any point the woman you knew as Elspeth Connor call herself by another name, in passing, or by mistake? Or maybe something she said didn't line up, or sounded off to you?"

Most of the dancers continued to shake their heads or just stare at him. Mrs. Connor sat down carefully in the nearest audience chair and twisted her handkerchief in her fingers.

One of the violinists in the orchestra pit raised his hand. He was a lanky young man with a dark mop of black hair and thick glasses. "I overheard her on the phone once. She mentioned something about a friend back home in Phoenix. I remember she said she was from Seattle, though. I wasn't trying to listen, I just overheard by accident."

Doyle sighed. "That's great, thank you. Anyone else hear something that might help us identify her?"

"Have you asked Abigail?" Penelope asked. "Her roommate would probably know the most about who she was."

"She's home sick today," Martha said. "Resting in bed."

"Okay, maybe there's something in Elspeth's things..." Doyle paused. "I mean, our victim's things that can help sort this out."

"I can go with you, let you in," Penelope said, then glanced at Arlena. She stood and slung her messenger bag over her shoulder.

"You're leaving?" Arlena asked.

Penelope nodded. "I need some air. And I want to check out the space we'll be working out of anyway, so I can let them into the building, so Martha and Armand don't have to. I'll be back to watch the show with you tonight."

"Okay," Arlena said. "You sure?"

"Yeah," Penelope said. "I want to see what it's like over there."

CHAPTER 23

Penelope walked with the Connors and Detective Doyle across to the apartment building, jaywalking halfway down the block during a break in traffic. Mrs. Connor hurried behind her husband, appearing fearful of the busy street.

Penelope used her key to open the outer lobby door, making sure it clicked shut behind them after they'd all entered the lobby. They stepped inside the elevator, and Penelope pressed the buttons for the twelfth and seventeenth floors.

Mr. Connor's body was ramrod straight, and anger radiated off of him like waves of heat. Mrs. Connor avoided looking directly at anyone, and stood cowering in the corner, her ever-present handkerchief shielding her face. Her faded red hair was tucked up under an antique looking hat, with a spray of green feathers glued to the rim. Penelope could see that beneath her mask of grief, she was quite lovely.

The doors rattled open on the twelfth floor, and Detective Doyle ushered the Connors out into the hallway, giving Penelope a small nod as the doors slipped closed again. Penelope rode up to the penthouse level, the elevator shifting slightly beneath her feet as it shuddered to a stop.

Stepping off the elevator, Penelope entered a wide-open space with a few desks and conference tables situated around the room. On the left was a doorway and an open island where a decent-sized, if a bit dated, kitchen sat. Penelope made her way over and sized it up, crossing her arms at her chest as she eyed the yellow Formica counters.

"This will be fine," she mumbled, picturing her chefs in the space. She was down to three on her team at the moment. The new chef she'd hired for a movie she'd catered in Vermont had decided to stay on there as head chef for a new restaurant owned by the film's director. That was the nature of the business sometimes, she knew.

Penelope turned and went to the windows, which lined the far wall, offering a pleasant view of the buildings across the street. She looked down at the Vitrine Theater, noticing for the first time the elaborate stone work on the building. There were comedy and tragedy masks on either end and gargoyles sneering down at the sidewalk from above. The glass office buildings on either side of the theater looked out of place next to the work of art in between them.

When Penelope looked into the small round attic windows of the theater, she noticed shadows moving across the glass. She leaned forward, her forehead almost touching the glass, and looked behind the theater at the alley. She was able to make out the edge of the black set piece boxes tucked behind the building, and the spot where Elspeth, or whatever the woman's name was, was found.

Penelope pulled her notepad from her bag and jotted down a few ideas about menus for the first couple of weeks, then set it down on the table behind her and sighed, deciding what to do next.

A quick tour of the rest of the apartment revealed two-bedroom suites on either side of the main room, both with bathrooms complete with a tub and shower. Perfect for a power nap between shows.

A few minutes later, Penelope pulled the door of the suite closed and got back on the elevator. She pulled out her phone to send a text to Arlena, looking up when the elevator came to a stop once again on the twelfth floor.

"That girl is lying, and you'd better find out—" Mr. Connor stopped speaking when he saw Penelope in the elevator, then sighed dramatically. "That's the thing about this city," he grumbled as he and his wife and Detective Doyle climbed inside, "you're never without a stranger looming over your every move."

"What makes you think she's lying?" Doyle asked.

"Obviously she knows more than she's saying," Mr. Connor sputtered. "You can see it all over her face."

"Okay," Doyle said, shooting Penelope a look of frustration as he jostled into place on the elevator.

Mrs. Connor clutched her purse with both hands, holding on so tight she caused the leather to strain as her husband kept his back to her.

Penelope reached into her messenger bag and plucked out a small packet of tissues. She reached over and handed them to Mrs. Connor.

The woman shook her head quickly and gave Penelope an angry glance, the first time she'd seen anything but sorrow from her. A second later she relented and accepted the tissues from Penelope.

"Was Abigail any help?" Penelope murmured to her.

Mr. Connor turned his head slightly, showing Penelope his red-rimmed ear.

"The girl is in shock, and she's quite unwell over it," Mrs. Connor said. "To her the young lady in the alley was Elspeth. She's as confused about all of this as we are."

"Hmph," Mr. Connor said. "I think she's in on whatever is happening."

"When's the last time you saw your daughter?" Penelope asked gently.

Mrs. Connor pressed a tissue beneath her eye. "Months ago now, the beginning of summer."

"Mr. Connor, we're going to have you come down and answer some more questions. Look through some photos," Detective Doyle said. "I'm going to request the theater hand over whatever photos or headshots they might have for all of the dancers who auditioned for the show."

"We'll do whatever it takes to find our daughter," Mrs. Connor said.

The elevator doors opened in the lobby and the Connors

hurried toward the door. Doyle held the door for Penelope just as her phone rang. She glanced at the screen and answered.

"Hi, Mrs. Sotheby." Doyle looked at her curiously as she stepped into the lobby. Penelope pressed the phone closer to her ear and smiled. "I'd love that. I'll ask Joey if that's a good day to join you."

Doyle nodded goodbye to her as she finished the call, then turned back toward the elevator. He looked back at her from the front door to the lobby and raised his eyebrows.

"I left something upstairs," she said, pressing the elevator button again. He raised his hand in a wave and stepped outside onto the sidewalk.

Stepping out onto the twelfth floor, Penelope could see it was much different from penthouse level. It looked much more like a typical city apartment building with doors on either side of a long-carpeted hallway. A sign pointed to A through D to the left, and E through H to the right. The rug in the hallway was a serpentine pattern that made her a little seasick if she looked at it for too long.

Penelope didn't know which apartment was Abigail's. So she decided to start with the first door and give it a knock. This building provided housing for the Big Apple Dancers, most of whom were across the street at rehearsal, so it would be a process of elimination.

The third one she tried was yanked open, even before she had a chance to pull her hand away.

"I told you—" Abigail said. When she saw Penelope she said, "Oh, hello. What are you doing here? You're the one from yesterday...the lady who found Elspeth."

"Yes, right. I'm sorry to bother you," Penelope said. "But I'm going to be working upstairs on seventeen for the next month or so and I was wondering..."

Abigail raised her eyebrows and leaned against her door.

"Do you know of a good place to get coffee near here?"

Penelope asked. "Not a chain, a local place if possible? Maybe organic?"

Abigail looked at her curiously. "There's the Urban Bean on the next corner over, facing Broadway."

"Oh that's perfect," Penelope said. She looked casually past Abigail into the small apartment.

"There's also this thing called Google," Abigail said. "You can type in 'coffee near me,' and find that kind of stuff out for yourself. You know, instead of knocking on every door in an apartment building."

Penelope smiled and shrugged, her cheeks blushing pink. "I like personal recommendations. Also, Martha said you were sick. I was checking to see if you needed anything. I could grab you some soup or something."

Abigail relented and gave her a small smile. "That's nice of you. Normally we have to scrounge for ourselves. Want to come in?"

"Sure," Penelope said. "I'm not intruding, am I?"

"Nah," Abigail said. "I'm going to have to start charging people to take a tour of my dead roommate's place."

"I saw the Connors leave," Penelope said distractedly. "I guess I'm a little curious about her too. I keep picturing her there in the alley." Penelope stepped inside the studio apartment. Two beds were pushed up against opposite walls, a kitchenette gleaming in the corner. A door inside the kitchen led to the bathroom, the claw foot of a tub just visible past the stove.

"I wish we'd had more time together," Abigail said. She plopped down on one of the bright orange bean bag chairs in the center of the floor and crossed her legs, her heels resting on opposite thighs. She wore bright white yoga pants and a slouchy black sweater, and no makeup. Even though she appeared delicate, like a porcelain doll, Penelope got the feeling underneath that fragile exterior she was tough as nails.

"This place is cute," Penelope said, sitting on the edge of one of the beds. The sheets were in a tumble like someone had jumped out of bed and hadn't taken the time to make it again.

Abigail sniffed. "I guess. It's convenient to work, at least. Zero minutes commuting back and forth."

"So you're under the weather today?" Penelope asked.

"I woke up with a fever, some kind of cold," Abigail said. "I'm still recovering from a pulled hamstring, too. After yesterday...Martha thought I should stay home. I wish I could sleep all day, but...it's too quiet here."

"Hopefully you'll be feeling better soon," Penelope said.

"Physically I'm sure I will. Mentally on the other hand..." Abigail said. "I should've stuck to beauty pageants, they're not as hard on the body. Or the mind."

"Can I ask you..." Penelope began cautiously. "What was Elspeth like?"

"You mean the girl who claimed to be someone else?" Abigail said weakly. Sweat made her forehead shiny and her eyes were weary. "I'm not sure what's been more traumatic: finding out my friend was killed or finding out my friend wasn't who she said she was."

"I know this must be hard. Why do you think she was pretending to be someone else?" Penelope asked.

Abigail shrugged her shoulders. "I have no idea. To me she was Elspeth. From Seattle. She liked sushi, and chai tea. I thought it was great, meeting someone from my home state all the way out here."

"You're from Seattle too?" Penelope asked.

"I never lived there but visited my cousins there a few times when I was younger." Abigail sighed and dropped her forehead in her hand.

"Did she ever say anything that made you think she wasn't from there?"

"No," Abigail said, considering. "We didn't talk too much about home, mostly about the show, the choreography, gossiped about the other girls. Not so much personal stuff."

"Hmm," Penelope said.

"One time she said something about Bucker's Diner near her school, but I thought that place closed years ago. She said she meant when she was younger, that I didn't hear her right, but I was pretty sure she was talking about high school, not elementary," Abigail said. "She changed the subject and ordered a pizza."

"Pizza?" Penelope asked, eyeing Abigail's long muscular legs.

"Yeah, she could eat," Abigail said. "Not that it showed up anywhere. Me, not so much. But I had a slice with her from time to time."

"So maybe this woman had lived in Seattle at some point in her life," Penelope said.

"Maybe. Or just visited. Or looked it up when she heard I was from there."

Penelope considered that as she glanced at the twisted sheets behind her on the bed. "She slept here?"

"Yep," Abigail said. "Cops took all her personal stuff. What little of it she had."

"Do you have any idea where Elspeth Connor is?" Penelope asked.

"That's the really weird part," Abigail said. She stretched her legs out and placed her bare feet on the floor in front of her. Penelope could see hard calluses on the edges of her toes. "If you're going to pretend to be someone else, why pick someone with a family, who will come looking for you? Why not just make up a new identity all together?"

"That's what the police need to find out," Penelope said. "And there's also a danger of the real Elspeth coming forward and exposing her." Penelope untangled the sheet, smoothing it out toward the pillow. A small dresser sat at the edge of the bed under the window and Penelope stood up and went over to it.

"That was hers, but like I said, they took everything," Abigail said.

Penelope slid open the top drawer, revealing nothing inside. The same for the next one down too. In the bottom drawer were a few coasters from different restaurants in the city.

"Those are from places she'd stopped in for a meal or a drink," Abigail said. "Her mementos, she called them. She liked to swipe coasters wherever she went."

Penelope picked one of them up, the cardboard slightly damp and warped between her fingers. "McNulty's."

"Touristy Irish bar around the corner," Abigail said. "There's only like thirty of those in the neighborhood."

Penelope knew she was exaggerating but she could see what Abigail meant.

"Do you feel safe here?" Penelope asked.

"Yeah. I'm hardly by myself," Abigail said. "I can see my work out my window, and this place is like a dormitory at night. Girls everywhere, coming and going from the apartments."

"So besides checking out local restaurants, what else did you guys do together?"

"Are you a chef or a detective?" Abigail said with a twist of her lip.

"Sorry, I'm just curious about her," Penelope said. "I don't mean to be nosy."

Abigail considered her for a moment and shrugged. "We didn't do anything secret or special. We danced, we slept, we rehearsed, we ate. That pretty much sums up the entire five weeks."

"Did you go anywhere besides places?" Penelope asked.

"Elspeth said she wanted to see the Statue of Liberty up close, you know, take that boat tour out there. And she went for runs around the reservoir in Central Park a couple of times. At least that's what she told me. Who knows now if that's what she was really doing."

Penelope sorted through the small stack of coasters she'd picked out of the drawer. "The Village Tavern. This place is in the park," she said under her breath.

"Oh yeah," Abigail said. "She stopped in there and swiped that one the day before...you know."

"She swiped it?"

"Yeah, she came home all worked up, said she'd ordered two

glasses of wine and ate lunch at the bar, then pretended she was going to the bathroom and pulled a dine-and-dash," Abigail said.

"Why would she do that?" Penelope asked.

Abigail shrugged. "I have no idea. Me and a lot of the other girls, we live pretty tight through the year. Getting a job dancing in a show doesn't pay a lot, unless you're at a certain level, or you become a Big Apple Dancer. This show pays well...well enough to not have to steal." Abigail tilted her head toward the windows in the direction of the theater. "Elspeth always seemed like she had money to spare, she treated me to dinner a couple of times."

Penelope turned the coaster over, considering.

"Elspeth came into town with money," Abigail offered. "At least it seemed that way to me. She never worried about it at all, and she was generous with all of us."

"If she had money, why not get a better apartment with more privacy?"

"I got the feeling she really liked being with the other girls," Abigail said. "If it were me, I wouldn't be cramped up in here, but I need the free room. If I had to pay rent in the city...I'd have to have two or three roommates at least."

"So there was no need for her to skip out on a check," Penelope said, holding up the coaster.

"I don't think so," Abigail said. "I think she did it for the thrill."

Penelope looked at the black and gold lettering on the coaster that spelled out The Village Tavern, one of New York's most celebrated restaurants, nestled in the green beauty of Central Park. And one of the last places Elspeth Connor's impersonator was seen alive.

CHAPTER 24

Penelope stood backstage with Arlena and watched the opening scenes of the Christmas Extravaganza. Watching the dancers from that vantage point was much different than when they'd been in the audience seats during rehearsal. The music sounded different, more muted. The orchestra pit was built to project the sound outward toward the audience.

"Aren't they wonderful?" Arlena whispered as she clasped her hands under her chin. Her diamond ring twinkled in the shadows thrown by the curtains where they stood backstage.

It was a sold-out show, all of the seats in the auditorium full of well-dressed theater goers. Many families with small children were in attendance, their little faces glowing from the stage light as they watched the magic unfold on the stage.

Armand and Randall watched from the opposite end of the stage. Arlena's father was just as mesmerized by the production as Arlena was, it seemed.

When the number ended, and the dancers hurried offstage to reset for the next scene, Arlena clapped along with the audience and said, "We're going to begin filming tomorrow," Arlena said. "The crew will report in first thing in the morning. I want to film rehearsal, behind the scenes stuff with the performers. You can be ready, right?"

Penelope nodded. "Absolutely. Sounds good, Director." Arlena leaned into her, tapping shoulder to shoulder.

The dancers moved into their places for the second number and the applause petered out. The music rose from the orchestra pit in a wave, washing over the audience as the Snow Queen made her first appearance on the stage.

Meredith had on her Christmas tree headdress and a long sequined gown with long slits on either side, revealing her long muscular legs beneath. She shimmered like nighttime snow in the moonlight as she made her way toward the front of the stage, the other dancers trailing her and matching her steps.

Penelope heard a pop somewhere overhead and she looked up, briefly dazzled by a stage light, that had swung downward and was now aiming right at them. Someone who appeared to be with the lighting crew scaled the rigging above the stage, stopping in front of a motherboard.

There was another pop from somewhere above and then suddenly the entire theater was plunged into darkness.

For a moment, the musicians continued, and the dancers stayed in their routine.

There were a few shouts from the audience, as the emergency lights came on, illuminating the edges of the aisles. Four exit signs glowed in the dark, two near the stage on either side, and two leading toward the lobby.

Armand looking up at the light tech, his palms raised in the air in a questioning manner.

Several more loud pops shattered the silence, followed by a pause and then more.

"Someone is shooting!" a man in the audience yelled. Several people screamed and began shouting as the patrons jumped to their feet.

Penelope's brain refused to let her think someone was shooting a gun inside the theater, with all of the children and innocent people present, but at the same time she couldn't think of what else could be happening.

The dancers rushed from the stage, stumbling over one another on their way to the exits. A few of the musicians leapt onto the stage from the pit, the lanky violinist who had spoken up the day before, helping one of the ladies to her feet after she twisted her ankle in the rush to escape.

"Come on," Arlena said, grabbing Penelope by the arm and pushing her toward the nearest exit.

Chaos broke out as everyone fled. Several people fell in their hurry to escape and were nearly trampled in the aisles.

The same loud pops sounded again. Something struck Penelope about the sound, how each time it was exactly the same pattern of pops.

Suddenly Randall was pulling the two of them behind a wall backstage.

"Are you okay?" he asked.

"What is going on, Daddy?" Arlena asked.

"It sounds like it's from up above," Penelope said, pointing to the scaffolding over their heads. The sound tech she'd noticed earlier was gone, but his headphones swayed at the end of a cord on the catwalk.

"Armand called the police," Randall said.

Just then the lights came back on in the theater. Many people had already made it through the exits, but Penelope could see a few people had stayed behind, crouching between the seats, unsure of what to do.

A shout came from up above and they all looked up.

Arlena put a hand over her mouth. A man fell to the stage and landed with a thud in the center of the floor and lay unmoving. It was the light tech Penelope had seen on the scaffolding.

Four police officers entered the theater from the main lobby and began ushering the remaining patrons outside. Penelope could see the officers were also looking around, sizing up the threat, trying to pinpoint exactly what was happening. Penelope rushed to the man on the stage as Randall waved the officers forward.

The light tech groaned and tried to lift his head.

"Try not to move," Penelope said urgently. His leg was pinned under him at an odd angle. She reached for his hand and placed hers gently on top of his. "Help is here."

"Bainbridge," he murmured, his eyes fluttering closed.

"Bainbridge."

Penelope heard sirens from outside. "They're here. You're going to be okay."

"I didn't think it was true. The ghost," the man said with a raspy chuckle. "This is what I get for not believing."

CHAPTER 25

In the aftermath of the incident, Penelope stood on the stage and stared at the personal debris left behind in the theater seats. Playbills littered the floor, items of clothing had been dropped in aisles. A tiny patent leather Mary Jane lay on its side near the front row.

"Who is this Bainbridge?" Detective Doyle asked, bringing her back to the present.

Penelope shrugged and shook her head. "They say there's a ghost who haunts the theater. That's who I think he was talking about."

"You said you saw him up on the scaffold before he fell?" Doyle asked.

"Yes," Penelope said. "I heard the first set of pops, and noticed him working on that big board up there."

"That's exactly what he was doing," Armand said, walking briskly toward them. His normal gentile manner was a bit frayed at the edges after the evening's events. "An unfortunate accident, his falling like that. He must have become disoriented when the lights were turned off."

"Did you blow a fuse?" Penelope asked.

"No, someone pulled the main switch and...poof," Armand said, splaying his fingers in the air.

"Are you sure that's what happened?" Doyle asked.

"Quite sure," Armand said.

"And what were those popping noises?" Penelope said.

Armand shrugged. "I heard them too. Whoever sabotaged our

show must have mimicked the sound of a gun to cause the most panic."

"My guys haven't found any sign of a shooter, or a gun," Detective Doyle said, motioning to the officers who were searching the main auditorium. "The only injuries so far from the theater goers are from falls. A few people got stepped on trying to get out. And an older lady broke her ankle in the rush out the door."

Armand put a hand on his forehead. "And my employee."

Doyle nodded. "If someone did this on purpose..."

"Why would someone do that?" Penelope asked. "Armand?"

"Who knows why people do anything these days? Who in their right mind would disrupt a holiday show—one that brings joy to families, in such a crass and terrible way—putting the lives of children in danger? I'm sure I don't know anyone like that."

"Okay, let's take this one step at a time," Doyle said. "Where is the main breaker for the theater, Mr. Wagner?" Doyle said.

"Right this way," Armand said, leading them further behind the scaffolding on the main floor. He pulled a set of keys from his pocket and chose a small one the size to fit a padlock.

The small gold lock dangled from the metal box, a shiny slice through the arm of it.

"You won't need that," Doyle said, bending at the waist slightly to eye the lock. "Someone has broken in."

CHAPTER 26

Arlena, Randall, and Penelope sat in silence at the large table in their suite across from the theater.

"What should we do?" Arlena asked.

Penelope folded her hands in her lap and looked down at them.

"We move forward with the project," Randall said. "That's my gut instinct."

"There was a murder, Daddy," Arlena said. "And now an accident during a show."

Penelope cleared her throat but otherwise stayed quiet.

"An even better reason to press forward," Randall said. "Maybe we add a true crime element to the documentary, cover the murder and blend it with the storyline of the history of the theater."

"What are you saying?" Arlena asked. She placed her elbows on the table and rested her chin in her palms.

"The death of the girl..."

"Jane Doe," Penelope interrupted. "They still haven't identified the woman pretending to be Elspeth Connor."

"Right," Randall said. "A mystery tied to the theater. I say we look into it, and maybe to some past incidents, for a more in-depth documentary."

"What other incidents?" Arlena asked.

Randall sighed and leaned back in his chair. "Aunt Tula told me Ruby died of a broken heart. But really, she died of an accidental overdose, maybe suicide. Sleeping pills and whiskey, is what my uncle told me. He made me promise not to say anything to

Tula, but wanted me to know when I got older, so I wouldn't start on the booze. I know Tula was trying to protect me, but...I think she Ruby got wrapped up with someone. A married guy, is my guess. A powerful married man."

"But what would her death that happened over forty years ago have to do with the woman in the alley?" Penelope asked.

"It's just the angle." Randall held his hands up wide, reading an invisible marquee between his thumbs. "Death visits the theater, past, present, future?"

"I spoke with Abigail again yesterday," Penelope said. "There might be more to Elspeth's story. She was into some weird behavior during her time in the city."

"Like what?" Randall asked.

"Stealing, for one thing," Penelope said. "She pulled a dine and dash at an upscale restaurant right before she was killed."

"Maybe she was broke, same as a lot of girls," Randall said. "Lots of them get here and don't realize how expensive just living here can be."

"But Abigail seemed to think she had money, that she wouldn't have to do something like that," Penelope said.

"That is strange then," Arlena said. "And who is she anyway? How can they not have figured that out yet? I mean, with DNA, fingerprints...still nothing?"

Penelope shrugged.

"I'd like to know how she got to be a Big Apple Dancer using someone else's identity," Penelope said.

Randall rubbed his hands together. "This is the real story of the Vitrine. We have to be investigative journalists on this one."

Arlena looked at her father with a wary glance, and then determination. "Okay. We look into the murdered girl in the alley and explore Ruby's death. The main storyline will center around the production and the theater itself, and how the culture here might impact the performers' lives."

"Do we tell Armand the focus?" Penelope asked.

"No," Randall said quickly. "This remains between us three.

We quietly pursue this story...you have a rapport with the roommate, so maybe you talk to her again, see what else you can dig up on our mystery woman. She already told you some very interesting things, maybe even more than she told the police."

Penelope nodded, a bit uncomfortable, but since she hadn't been directly asked to do anything she felt was out of her realm of ability, she kept quiet.

"Arlena carries on with the documentary filming," Randall said. "We film the shows, we talk to the girls, but we keep in mind we're looking for anything that might tie into our focus. I'll keep funding the project. The donation I gave the theater was very much appreciated, so that will buy us some flexibility, as far as our presence during the shows."

"And what are you going to do?" Arlena asked.

"I'm going to find out what happened to my mother," Randall said.

CHAPTER 27

The next morning Arlena and Penelope rode into the city early together, sitting in the back of a large black SUV. Randall had sent a car service for them, so they wouldn't have to worry about parking or taking the train. When they arrived on Forty-Fifth Street, Penelope saw the nose of her kitchen truck pointing out from the alley. Francis was at the wheel, slowly backing the vehicle between the buildings, edging it along carefully so as not to scrape the paint.

"Hey, Boss," Francis said after he put the truck in park and hopped out. "Nice spot, huh?"

Penelope smiled. "Have you seen the paper this morning?"

"No," Francis admitted. "What, they did a write-up on us already? Red Carpet Catering live in Manhattan?"

"Um, no," Penelope said. "There was an incident at the theater."

"Oh man," Francis said, his smiling face morphing to concern. "You okay, Boss?"

"I'm okay," Penelope said. "Some strange things have been happening around here, is all."

"I heard about the girl," Francis said. He looked at the alley behind the truck then back at her. "They said to park here, so..."

"Yeah," Penelope said. "It's okay."

"Feels weird, though, right?" Francis asked.

"Yeah, it does."

A homeless man shuffled past them on the sidewalk, mumbling to himself. He had what looked like a tarp on top of his head, which Penelope thought must be a plastic sheet cut into a makeshift raincoat. A wiry gray and black beard obscured the rest of his face.

After he got a few yards away Penelope said, "There's a shelter on the next block. Keep an eye out on the truck, you know."

"Yeah," Francis said. "Understood."

"And whatever we have leftover each day, if we can't use it again, let's go see if they want it, okay?"

"Sure thing."

"Okay, so the other guys are on their way in. What else do you need from me?" Penelope asked.

"We're good, Boss," Francis said. "Your text said the office is up there, right?"

Francis shielded his eyes from the sun and looked up at the building across the street.

"Yeah, we're on the top."

The front door of the building opened and three of the dancers stepped outside, pulling their jackets closer in the cold winter air.

"They live there too, huh?" Francis said, eyeing the women as they headed to the coffee shop on the corner.

"Yes," Penelope said. "I hope you don't find that too distracting."

"Nah," Francis said. "Not at all. It's New York, there are beautiful women on every corner."

Penelope gave him a stern look and slapped him lightly on the shoulder. "Okay, get going. I'll be upstairs if you need me. Oh, here's your key."

"Got it," Francis said, taking the set from her. His eyes drifted toward the coffee shop again.

"You want a coffee?" Penelope asked.

"Let me go get you some," Francis offered quickly.

Penelope chuckled. "Okay, fine. My usual. Bring it up, will you?"

"You got it," Francis said as he hurried away.

Penelope watched him go for a minute then shook her head before heading up to the suite.

CHAPTER 28

Up in the suite, Penelope made some notes. Using the notebook, she normally carried for recipes and menu planning she'd begun a new page with notes about Elspeth Connor, Abigail Hamilton and a question mark to represent the woman found in the alley.

Pulling out her iPad, she googled Elspeth. She sighed when she discovered she had no social media accounts, or at least any under her name that Penelope could find. A news article came up from the *Seattle Times* featuring a group photograph of a high school dance troupe where Elspeth was listed along with several other girls. Penelope enlarged the photo, focusing in on her face. She had a shy smile, long red hair and fair skin. The girls stood ramrod straight in a line, decreasing in size from the middle down each side in order of height. She resembled the woman in the alley, but there were differences too. Elspeth had plumper cheeks, and her eyes were set closer together. It also appeared she might have had freckles, if the black and white picture wasn't playing tricks on her eyes.

Penelope then turned to the news, looking for any updates on the case. The main story, of course, was the incident at the Vitrine the night before, and the member of the crew being involved in an accident during the show. There was no mention of anyone tampering with the light box, and she wondered if Armand had pulled any strings to keep that news out of the paper.

She sat back in her chair and thought. Who would have been able to get to the power box and cut the lights during the show? It had to have been someone with knowledge of the theater's layout, who came prepared to cut the lock. She didn't imagine a patron would have been able to get backstage and go unnoticed.

The sidebar article was about the death in the alley, and Penelope clicked on it. They still hadn't identified the victim. A computerized photo of her face was included with the article and Penelope stared at it, her hollow cheeks and thin lips, her narrow almond-shaped eyes, that were light brown, almost the same color as her hair. A tip line number was printed below the graphic, urging people to come forward with any information about the woman.

Penelope stood up and stretched, then went to her coat, which she'd slung over one of the dining room chairs. Reaching inside one of the pockets for the stack of coasters Abigail had let her take from her apartment, her fingers brushed against a small piece of metal.

She pulled out the item, remembering the star-shaped medal she'd found in the coat closet at the theater. She held it up to get a better look, noticing it was tarnished and brassy, the design a star within a star. Walking back to the table she set it down, then spread the stack of coasters onto the table.

Picking up one after the other, she made a list, looking up the addresses for a few of them. The elevator pinged faintly outside in the hallway off the suite.

"There you are," Arlena said as she came through the door.

"Hey," Penelope said, setting down her pen. "Just doing a little research."

"Everything coming along well?" Arlena asked.

"I'm thinking of it as *mise en place*," Penelope said, nodding. "Everything in its place. The secret of all great chefs. Before you begin, get yourself organized."

"If everything could only be that easy," Arlena said. She took a seat at the table and crossed her arms.

"What's up?" Penelope asked.

"Do you feel like I'm doing too much? I mean, this movie with Daddy, and I have a wedding to plan..."

"I think you can do whatever you think you can do," Penelope said. "I can help with the wedding, you know. Come up with a menu. I worked a few nice ones between semesters in culinary school."

"I know. I don't want to ask too much of you," Arlena said, shaking her head.

"Have you set a date yet?"

"Not yet," Arlena admitted.

"Then it's up to you. Maybe put off the planning until after this project?" Penelope said.

"You're the most rational person I know," Arlena said with a laugh. "I don't have to drive myself crazy."

"Exactly," Penelope said.

"Anyway, back to the work at hand...the crew will be here soon to set up, and I've got some interviews with the performers before the show."

"They're going forward with the shows today?" Penelope asked. "I mean, after last night?"

Arlena shrugged. "They didn't cancel them. I'm not sure how many people might not show up because of last night, but as far as I know they're pressing on as planned. Armand said it was probably a prank."

"Pretty stupid prank, and dangerous," Penelope said darkly.

"I know," Arlena said. "I get the idea that they can't lose the revenue by cancelling shows. I'm not sure what they would've done if Daddy hadn't come along with his influx of cash."

The door opened and Francis entered, carrying a cardboard drink container with a few coffees tucked inside.

"Good coffee run?" Penelope teased.

"Yeah," Francis said. "I brought a few."

"Excellent," Penelope said.

"That block is weird," Francis said.

"How's that?" Arlena asked.

"It's a mix of beautiful women at the theater, then an office building full of accountants next door, and a bunch of homeless dudes thrown in for flavor," Francis said.

Penelope got up and looked out the window at the theater, then down the block toward the shelter, then the other way toward the coffee shop. Commuters walked quickly down the street, heading off for their day or to the subway station that was two blocks away on Broadway.

"Hey where did you get the service medal?" Francis asked, picking up the small emblem from the table.

"That's what that is?" Penelope asked.

"Yeah, my grandfather had one of these," Francis said. "From his time in Vietnam."

"I found it at the theater," Penelope said. "When I was locked in the coat closet."

"Probably fell out of someone's jacket," Arlena said. "Armand probably has a lost and found."

"Good idea," Penelope said. She remembered the closeness of the closet, the momentary panic she'd felt inside. She slipped the medal into the pocket of her jeans and reminded herself to bring it to lost and found the next time she was inside the theater.

The small round windows on the top floor of the theater reflected the morning sunlight. Penelope thought about all of the people who had passed through its doors, their dreams of dancing on Broadway coming true, and all the joy they had given audiences over the years.

A shadow cut across one of the windows, and Penelope focused on it. A pigeon landed on the roof above it and fluttered its wings, then took flight, its shadow momentarily darkening the glass with its reflection.

Penelope watched the bird fly higher into the sky and took a deep breath. Something moved behind one of the attic windows again and Penelope saw someone staring back at her from the attic.

CHAPTER 29

"In the attic," Penelope said. "I saw someone up there."

"From across the street?" Armand asked doubtfully. He sat behind his desk in his office that hovered above the stage. Penelope was still catching her breath after hurrying over and climbing the stairs to find him dining on a croissant and latte at his desk. "Are you sure?"

"Yes," Penelope said. "At first, I thought it was a shadow, or the reflection of a pigeon on the roof, but then I saw him. There was someone up there, I know it. Who else is here right now?"

"Only me, unless someone from the crew decided to come in early. But no one really goes up there," Armand said. "I've got the only key to the top floor. It's just storage, and the archives."

"Then you should definitely have a look, if you haven't been up there yourself this morning," Penelope said. "What if someone is hiding up there? Or it's whoever pulled that prank last night?"

Armand sat up straighter at that. "All right then, I suppose we should check it out."

"We?" Penelope said.

"Oh you must come with me," Armand said. "I want you to show me exactly what you saw."

Penelope followed Armand up a back staircase from the apartment suite attached to his office, through a hatch in the rear bedroom. When they opened the hatch, a bit of dust fell in on them.

"See, my dear?" Armand said. "No one has been up there in weeks."

Penelope's confidence in what she had seen slipped as they

climbed into the attic. Armand flipped on the light switch and several bulbs suspended from the rafters came on, although the morning sun illuminated enough to show Armand was probably right, the attic was an abandoned space.

A dressmaker dummy had been pushed up against one of the walls near the window. Penelope's cheeks reddened when she saw it, and imagined how the daylight may have been playing tricks with her eyes.

"I guess I imagined it," Penelope sighed. "Sorry to drag you up here."

"Not a problem at all, my dear," Armand said, placing his hands in his suit jacket pockets.

"How is your injured crew member?" Penelope asked.

"He has a broken leg and a fractured wrist," Armand said. "He's fortunate he fell the way he did."

"Did he say anything about what happened?" Penelope asked.

"Only kept repeating that Bainbridge pushed him," Armand said with a shake of his head.

"Isn't that the ghost?" Penelope asked.

"One in the same. You can see why I'm skeptical."

"You don't believe in Bainbridge?" Penelope asked.

"I'm afraid I don't," Armand said. "I find human beings are perfectly capable of causing all the mayhem on earth we require."

Penelope walked to the dress form and put a hand on it, feeling the polyester material beneath her fingers. The toe of her boot tapped a box against the wall, and Penelope crouched down to open it.

"Oh my," Penelope said.

"What is it?" Armand asked.

"Maybe I'm not crazy after all," she said, plucking out a small picture.

Holding it up for Armand to see, she said, "This was the photo that was taken from my wallet the first day we were here."

"I stand corrected," Armand said. "It appears we have an intruder in the attic!"

"But how do you suppose he gets up here?" Armand asked, eyeing the neglected space around them.

Penelope looked at the floor, and saw that some of the dust had been trodden through, leading to one of the windows facing the rear alley of the theater. She went over and pressed on the window frame.

"This one is loose," Penelope said, swinging it outward.

"I suppose our ghost in the attic could squeeze through there, if he wasn't too large," Armand said.

"I think you could make it," she said, eyeing his slender frame.

"I would probably get stuck," Armand said, patting his flat stomach. "I suppose I should call Detective Doyle." Armand wrung his hands. "I fear all this commotion won't be good for the Vitrine. I wouldn't want word to get out some ghoul was pillaging our patrons' personal items while they're trying to enjoy a night at the theater."

Penelope went back to the box and looked again. "Nothing in here looks all that valuable," she said. "It's all personal things: photos, and trinkets, souvenirs you could get anywhere."

"Then why run the risk of taking them at all?" Armand said in exasperation.

"When we figure that out, we'll be closer to finding your squatter."

CHAPTER 30

Detective Doyle looked up at the fire escape snaking down the back of the theater into the alley and nodded.

"I suppose that's how he gets up there," Doyle said, shielding his eyes from the sunlight. "Tell me again exactly what you saw."

Penelope related the events of that morning, including finding the dress form near the window. When she finished she asked, "Detective, have you gotten any closer to figuring out the name of the woman in the alley?"

"Not yet," Doyle said, shaking his head. "We've had hundreds of calls, most of them dead ends, or people who have a family member missing, some who look nothing like our victim."

"Elspeth was from the west coast," Penelope said. "Have you received any tips from the Seattle area?"

"A couple," Doyle said. "We're still sorting through everything. Nothing solid yet."

Penelope bit her bottom lip and pulled on the lapels of her pea coat. "My team will be cooking here starting today. Feel free to stop by whenever you're here...working."

"Thanks," Doyle said, with a surprised glance. "Hey, did I hear you correctly the other day on the phone. You know someone named Sotheby?"

Penelope smiled. "I do, a good friend. Older lady."

"Not the auction place, right?" he asked with a chuckle.

"No, a retired school teacher," Penelope said.

"It's just that," Doyle began, then paused. "That name rings a bell. If she's a teacher we might know the same family."

"Oh yeah?" Penelope asked. "How do you know her?"

"Well, I didn't know them," Doyle said. "But my first partner when I made detective, that was his bottom drawer case. Talked about it a few times with me."

"Bottom drawer?" Penelope asked.

"Yeah, every detective has a case they keep in their bottom desk drawer. I got a couple of my own, trails gone cold, the ones you can't solve no matter how much you try."

"Don't they have cold case departments now, that look into cases like that?" Penelope asked.

Doyle chuckled. "Are you a big fan of cop shows or something?"

"My boyfriend is a detective in New Jersey," Penelope said. "I hear about things from him sometimes."

"That makes sense," Doyle said.

"This case of your partner's," Penelope said. "Was it a shooting? A man buying flowers, and the clerk gunned down on a Thursday afternoon in the city?"

"That's the one," Doyle said. "No witnesses, the customer and the owner the only two people in the store. And the mutt who shot them both. From what they could tell he got twenty-three dollars from the till. I think that's what sent my partner over the edge, how little the perp thought the lives were worth of those two men."

"That's my friend's husband," Penelope said. "The customer. Did your partner have any suspicions about who did it?"

"He had a couple of suspects," Doyle said with a nod. "But no proof to tie any of them to the crime. He'd be sure it was one of them, then be just as sure about another one. That's how it went with him."

"What's your partner doing now?" Penelope asked. She glanced at Doyle's graying hair and mustache and tried to work out how many years he'd been a detective. She thought Doyle might be close to retirement himself, but she didn't want to ask and possibly offend him.

"He passed away fifteen years ago now," Doyle said with a

shake of his head. "He was my age when we partnered up. Back then they put the new guys with someone who knew the ropes, although that theory is out of practice now. Sometimes the old dogs show you the wrong ways, you know? Not always, but sometimes."

"So no one has looked into Mr. Sotheby's murder since?" Penelope asked.

"I doubt it," he said. "Look, I should be going, but call me if anything comes up, okay? I caught a double homicide yesterday, a couple of guys decided to shoot at each other over drugs in some abandoned building a few blocks toward the river."

"I didn't see anything about it in the paper," Penelope said, thinking back.

Doyle shrugged. "It's not a high profile case. Gang stuff, your everyday run of the mill transaction gone bad. When a white woman is murdered or goes missing, it's on the front page. These guys probably don't get a mention."

Penelope watched him go, thinking about all the things he'd seen during his career, all the bloodshed and heartache. Then she thought about Joey, growing old with him, and whether he'd be able to keep his playfulness after years of investigating what sometimes came from people acting at their worst.

Doyle knocked on the side of her food truck on his way out of the alley. "Got your permits in order?" he called jokingly over his shoulder.

"Oh, yes," Penelope said with a smile. "Always."

CHAPTER 32

Penelope worked side by side with Francis in the truck for a few hours, prepping for lunch, which they planned to serve during rehearsal. She had decided the kitchen space in the theater was too small to be functional, so they'd just use it as their staging area. It was near the dressing rooms where the performers would be taking breaks anyway. She'd also decided to set up a couple of tables backstage for the other techs and the musicians, so the women wouldn't have to worry about the male crew members walking through when they might be changing.

When they had everything well underway and her other two chefs had arrived to help set up inside, she turned to Francis and put a hand on his shoulder. "I've got an errand to run, but I'll be back in about an hour. I'm on my cell if anything comes up." Francis nodded and she turned on the radio for him. When she stepped down from the truck she looked in through the window and saw his head bobbing to the music.

Penelope skipped down the subway steps on the next corner, swiping her fare card and hurrying through the turnstile and onto a waiting uptown train. A few stops later she jogged up the concrete steps and took a left, heading for the restaurant that sat on the edge of Central Park.

The Village Tavern was decorated for the holidays with silver and gold ornaments hanging from the high ceilings, and gold chargers and flatware on the white tablecloths. The dining room to the left of the entrance was full, the familiar sound of forks tapping against china plates ringing in the air.

"Do you have a reservation?" the woman in the tight black dress behind the podium asked, eyeing Penelope's jeans and boots beneath her peacoat. She was a pro, Penelope thought, because her expression remained neutral.

"Sorry, no," Penelope said. "I was just stopping in for a drink on the way home from work."

The hostess smiled and flicked her eyes toward the next room. "The bar's just through there. Can I take your coat?"

"No thanks," Penelope said, "I'll hang onto it."

The hostess set her mouth in a line and nodded.

"Welcome to the Tavern," she said, suddenly distracted by an elderly couple stepping up behind her.

Penelope slipped away as she greeted the more appropriately dressed guests.

The bar was horseshoe shaped, protruding out into the rear dining area. The walls were all glass looking out onto the park, providing a lovely view during any season of the year. Penelope chose a stool and slipped off her coat, hanging it on the back of it. Cocktail menus had been placed in between every third seat or so, and she picked one up, marveling at the prices listed next to the drinks. She tapped her finger on the mahogany, smiling when a good-looking bartender emerged from a swinging door behind the bar.

"Welcome to the Tavern," he said in the exact same manner as the hostess, "What can I get for you?"

"I'll have a glass of the Pinot," she said, pointing to an entry on the wine list in her hand. She thought about getting a glass of water or tea, but thought getting a drink that had a nicer tip attached to it would work better at getting his attention.

"Anything for lunch?" he asked, as he poured the ruby liquid into an elegant stemmed glass.

"Not quite yet," Penelope said, taking a sip of wine.

"Okay, well, let me know when you're ready. Name's Derek." He turned and tapped on the register a few times.

"I did want to ask you something, though," Penelope said,

setting down her glass.

"They're not hiring right now, as far as I know."

"Oh, right," Penelope said. "Actually I was curious to see if you remembered someone I heard was in here recently."

"Oh," Derek said. The ticket machine next to the register spit out a piece of paper. "One second."

Penelope watched him mix a Manhattan straight up and a dirty martini, then place them on a round serving tray for one of the waitress.

"So," he said, heading back to her. "Who are you curious about? The Clooneys? The Seinfelds? Kelly Ripa lives down the street, I've heard. Who are you interested in stalking?"

"It's nothing like that," Penelope said with a laugh. "I heard that there was a young woman in here who skipped out on her tab, maybe some time last week?"

"Oh, yeah," Derek said, rolling his eyes. "The artist."

"Artist?" Penelope asked.

"That's what she said she was," he said with a grimace. "She came on to me. Hard. And then skipped out on the tab."

Penelope took another sip of wine and the ticket machine whirred again. He grabbed two rocks glasses from a shelf above the register and filled them with ice, pouring sour mix and whiskey inside a shaker. He placed the drinks on another small tray, garnishing both with lemon twists.

When he turned back to Penelope she said, "Did the woman have red hair and green eyes?" Penelope asked, pulling out her phone. She pulled up the computer sketch from the newspaper she had saved to her images.

"That's her," Derek said. "That's not a good photo of her though. She's a knockout. What's with all the questions? I didn't press charges or anything."

"I'm just curious about who she was," Penelope said.

"What do you mean was?" he asked.

Penelope turned the picture toward him again. "She was found murdered in the Theater District."

"Oh," he said, his face going pale. "I heard something about that...that was her?"

"Afraid so," Penelope said.

"Man, I had no idea," he said. "Are you a journalist?"

"No," Penelope said. "No, but I'm...connected to her. Can you think of anything else that stuck out about her?"

"Well, when she was pouring it on with the flirting, I did catch her in a lie."

"Really?" Penelope asked, sitting up straighter. "What was it?"

"The usual way you trap someone when you think they're giving you a snow job," he said.

"I'm not sure what you mean."

"I asked her where she lived. She said in Midtown. I told her I used to work at Murphy's Pub on Seventh. She said she knew the place."

"And..."

"I made it all up," he said in a whisper. "I'm a good actor."

"Right," Penelope said. "Did she introduce herself by name?"

The bartender put his hands on his hips and looked at the ceiling, thinking. "I don't remember. She got the better of me. I should've known better than to...I shouldn't have trusted her."

"You can't always tell when someone is going to skip," Penelope said. "She was just a stranger like everyone else at your bar."

"I'm smarter than that, shouldn't have fallen for her scam," Derek said. "I had to pay her tab myself so I wouldn't get written up."

"Did she say anything else that was, I don't know, weird or might give a clue as to who she is?" Penelope asked.

"Not that I can remember," Derek said. "She said she was wealthy, which is hilarious because, why skip if you have money? She was gorgeous too. Great body." He shook his head.

"Did she tell you she was a dancer, appearing in the Christmas Extravaganza?" Penelope asked.

"No, but that makes sense," he said. "She was in the kind of shape those girls have to be in, you know?"

"I've been around them recently, so I do know what you mean," Penelope said.

"This girl, though," Derek said, an odd look coming into his eyes. "She wasn't as hard. There was a softness to her."

Penelope stared at him.

"You know what, I'm sorry that someone...I'm sorry this happened. She seemed nice, even though she ripped me off."

"And you never saw her before that day at the bar?"

Derek shook his head. "Last thing I saw, she was chatting up one of our regulars. Hitting on him pretty hard, too."

Penelope took another sip of wine. "Did he seem interested in her?"

"Nah," he said. "She was barking up the wrong tree with that guy. He's got a husband and a couple of kids at home."

He wiped a spot of water from the bar. "You have to be careful who you talk to in this town. She seemed to not understand that. It's not like home, where everyone knows your business."

"Home?"

"You know, everyone comes here from all these small towns. They get to the city and think they're going to be treated a certain kind of way because they have a talent, or they're beautiful. It's much more competitive here. They can't always handle it."

"Are you from the city?"

"Upstate. You?"

"Jersey."

The ticket machine went again and Derek tossed a towel onto the bar, a bit of frustration showing through his friendly demeanor. "She didn't deserve to get killed. Even if she was a liar and a cheat."

Penelope finished her wine and paid her tab, slipping a twenty into the little leather folder before heading back out into the cold.

CHAPTER 33

"Abigail," Penelope said when she got back to the theater. Abigail was sitting in one of the chairs outside the dressing rooms, staring at her phone. "You back to work today?"

"Just sitting in on rehearsal to watch," she said. "I'm not cleared to dance yet."

"I just came from the Tavern," Penelope said. "Met the bartender your roommate skipped out on."

"Really?" Abigail said, perking up.

"Yeah," Penelope said. "She seemed to make an impression on him."

"I can see that," Abigail said. "She had one of those magnetic personalities."

"This guy made her out to be quite a flirt."

Abigail shot her a glance. "Sometimes guys think you're coming on to them when all you're doing is being nice. Lots of creeps out there," she muttered.

"Do you think she came from money?"

Abigail chewed her lip. "Not really. She told me she went to public school in Seattle, and went to school on a dance scholarship."

"Was she a good dancer?"

"She was okay," she said, lowering her voice. "She seemed to be getting the hang of it."

"But she made the audition, so she must be good," Penelope said.

"It's funny," Abigail said. "She came out to audition and got the spot, but then it was like...I don't know. She was always really nervous during rehearsal. Like she'd miss steps and stuff. She was always practicing up in the apartment."

"Maybe because it was her first big show," Penelope asked. "I still get nervous sometimes when I first get on a new movie set."

"Maybe it was something like that," Abigail said. "It's hard to explain, but she went from totally confident the first day to almost having stage fright a week later, major anxiety before each rehearsal."

Penelope sighed and sat down in the chair next to Abigail. "I'm so confused," she said. "You guys work so hard to get to this stage. If Elspeth wasn't Elspeth, how did she get to be good enough to get a spot here?"

Abigail shrugged. "She was just as good as me. Not the best but better than most. Dancing isn't brain surgery, you can do anything if you practice hard enough."

"I'm just wondering," Penelope said, "if she was pulling some kind of scam or using someone else's identity. But you can't fake talent, right?"

"Right," Abigail said. "Not at this level. Whoever she was, she had some dance training somewhere. And she probably worked her ass off after that."

Penelope's phone buzzed in her back pocket, an unknown number with a New York area code flashed on the screen.

"Oh hi, Detective," Penelope said. "How did you get my number?"

"That's the thing. I found your business card."

"Okay..." Penelope said, confused. She couldn't remember giving him one, or her number either.

"Your card was in a woman's pocket," Doyle said.

Penelope pressed the phone closer to her ear.

"Someone killed her," Doyle said quietly.

Penelope put her palm to her forehead and stared at Abigail.

"Who is she? Please, who did you find?" Penelope asked, her voice getting louder. She thought about all the people she'd handed a business card to, unable to guess who he might be talking about.

"She's a homeless woman, who stays at the shelter down the street from the theater most of the time," Doyle said.

"Oh no," Penelope said. It felt like her heart was beating out of her chest. "What happened?"

"She was stabbed and strangled," Doyle said. "I'm sorry to have to tell you this, but I wanted you to know, and I'd like to come by and ask you a few more questions."

"Of course," Penelope said. "Wait, strangled and stabbed. Just like Elspeth."

"True," Doyle said. "I'm sure I don't have to remind you to be careful."

"I hear it every day from my boyfriend," Penelope said.

Doyle sighed. "We're working with the shelter to identify our victim. Do you remember giving your card to anyone recently?"

Penelope shook her head, even though he couldn't see her, the shock of hearing the news ebbing away. "I've given out hundreds of cards, Detective. My crew too."

"But no homeless people that you can remember?"

Penelope thought again. "There was a woman and her daughter a few days ago, but that was near my home in New Jersey."

"Okay," Doyle said. "Would you mind coming down to the station? I know you're busy but it would really help if we could identify this victim, see if there's any connection to our first victim."

"It seems like the connection might be me," Penelope said.

"One thing at a time," Doyle said softly. "I'll text you the address. Watch your back in the meantime."

"Thanks, Detective," Penelope said numbly. "I'll be right down."

CHAPTER 34

Penelope walked into the three-story gray building on West End Avenue and presented her ID at the security desk. The woman behind the glass eyed her license for longer than Penelope thought was usual, then handed it back to her. Her fingernails were so long Penelope wasn't sure how she could type on the keyboard in front of her, but after a few clicks, Detective Doyle opened the secured door and showed her inside.

"Thanks for coming down so quickly," Doyle said. He handed her a plastic evidence bag with her card inside.

"Of course," Penelope said. "I just hope I can be of help."

"This is what we found," Doyle said. His shoulders drooped and Penelope noticed his stomach protruded slightly over his belt. They stepped into an elevator and went down a level to the basement.

Penelope turned it over, smoothing the bag over two scrawled names: *Chadwick* and *Connor* had been written in blue pen. The card was worn, like it had been in the woman's pocket continuously for days. "Did you see these?"

"Yes," Doyle said with a nod. "Obviously we know the Connors. Still trying to find a link to Chadwick."

"Maybe it's a clue to the woman in the alley?" Penelope asked.

"Possibly," Doyle said. "Or the name of a place, or who knows what it could be? We are checking into it, but it's like a needle in a haystack if we have nothing to check the name against."

When the doors opened, the smell of antiseptic and lemon floor cleaner assaulted her nose and she put a hand over her mouth.

"You okay?" Doyle asked, appearing to not notice the odor.

Penelope nodded and kept her hand in place as she followed him down a corridor to the left. They stopped outside a glass window, and Doyle rapped on it gently.

A few minutes later the blinds were drawn up and a man wearing a lab coat was visible on the other side.

"We've identified her through fingerprints, corroborated by the staff at the shelter. Our victim had an extensive sheet, mostly minor offences, panhandling, vagrancy, a couple of solicitation busts going back thirty years. She spent a couple of months behind bars for theft. Oranges, from a grocery store. Back in the zero tolerance era where people like her would get locked up for anything."

"What's her name?" Penelope asked.

"Gabby Bainbridge. AKA Mother, according to the director at the shelter."

Doyle nodded at the coroner on the other side of the glass. A gurney holding a zipped black body bag rolled to the window and Penelope held her breath as the tech unzipped it.

"Is that the woman from the grocery store?" Doyle asked. "The one you gave your card to?"

"Yes," Penelope said, dropping her hand from her mouth. A lump formed in the back of her throat and she swallowed it back down. "Where did you find her?"

"Just a few blocks from the theater, in an alley behind a dry cleaner," Doyle grumbled.

"Did you say her name was Bainbridge?"

"That's correct," Doyle said, looking down at the notes in his hand.

"That's the name of the ghost at the Vitrine," Penelope said.

"I'm sorry, a ghost?"

"Some legend about the theater being haunted. One of the original lead actors died during a production. They say his ghost haunts the theater."

Doyle sighed. "It's interesting the names are the same. Can you tell me exactly what your encounter was like? Why did you give her your business card?"

"Gabby was with another woman. I thought it was her daughter, because she kept calling her Mother. There was something wrong with their debit card, or whatever, and they couldn't pay for their groceries. I went ahead and covered it. Gabby insisted on getting my information so she could pay me back, even though I insisted they didn't have to do that."

Doyle gave her a smile. "That was kind of you."

Penelope shrugged. "Anyone would've done the same thing."

"I'm not so sure about that," Doyle said.

"Detective, who would do this?" Penelope asked.

Doyle put a hand lightly on her shoulder. "I'm working on it, I promise. Let's go outside, get some air."

Penelope nodded gratefully. "Wait, what about the other...aspect of the attack?"

"What do you mean?"

"Was she...attacked sexually?" Penelope asked.

"There's no clear evidence of sexual activity," Doyle said.

"That's a relief."

Doyle led Penelope back to the elevators and outside the front door of the station. She breathed in the fresh air, relived to be free from the bowls of the police station. "Do you think it's the same killer?"

Doyle considered the question before answering. "Gabby Bainbridge was dumped behind the dry cleaner, stuffed inside a large cooler, roughly the same size as the case we found our first victim in."

"So they must be connected," Penelope said.

Doyle nodded, his face grim. "So far it appears that way. And they're both connected to the theater. And you."

"Me?"

Detective Doyle pulled an envelope from his back pocket and handed it to Penelope. Her name was scrawled in blue ink on the front.

"What's this?" Penelope asked, taking it from him.

"It was found in Elspeth's belongings," Doyle said. "A letter addressed to you, Penelope Sutherland of Red Carpet Catering."

She shook her head. "I've never met her. I would've remembered by now, her name is unusual."

"Either way, she seems to have known about you," Doyle said.

Penelope pulled the document from the envelope. "It's Elspeth's résumé?" Penelope asked. "She wanted to be a chef?"

"Apparently," Doyle said. "Are you hiring?"

"Yes," Penelope said. "I mean, I'm always on the lookout for talented people."

"You know many professional dancers who are also chefs?"

"No, but it's not the craziest thing I've ever heard," Penelope said. "It says here she studied culinary arts in Portland, Oregon. Maybe she was looking for a fallback career?"

"Seems to me Elspeth wasn't old enough to have one career yet, much less a second one."

"I checked with that school," Doyle said. "They don't have a record of her attending. Do you check references when you hire new chefs?"

"Always," Penelope said. "I would've found out she wasn't qualified. So why bother?"

CHAPTER 35

Penelope sat in Detective Doyle's cramped office waiting for him to return from getting them each a cup of coffee. Papers were stacked on his metal footed desk and a newer looking file cabinet sagged under more files in the corner.

"Here you go," Detective Doyle said, handing her a blue and white paper cup. "It doesn't look like much, but it's actually pretty good. Will warm you up, at least."

Penelope held the cup in both hands, savoring the heat radiating into her palms.

"Nothing came up when you ran the girl from the alley's fingerprints through the system?" Penelope asked.

"No hits," Doyle said, sitting down heavily in his chair.

"There are dozens of catering companies in New York," Penelope said. "Not to mention restaurants, clubs, thousands of other places for her to work. Why pick me?"

"How would she find out about your company?" Doyle asked.

"Well, every job we do, we get a credit on the movie. I'm listed as head chef, and then the members of my team. If you're one of those people who stay for the end of the credits, that's where we're listed."

"Uh huh," Doyle said.

"And Red Carpet Catering is named as a choice of employer with many of the hospitality and culinary schools," Penelope said. "Companies like mine are always looking for talented candidates."

"But why you?" Detective Doyle said after a sip of coffee. "Like you said, it's not like you're the only game in town."

"That's what makes me think there's something more, like Elspeth wanted to meet me for another reason all together. Or..."

"Or what?"

"Maybe the Madisons," Penelope said. "I work for a pretty famous family. If for some reason she wanted to try and meet them, it's possible she'd choose my company to apply."

"Possibly," Doyle said, jotting something on a pad. "Tell me, do you have future projects listed anywhere?"

"Yes," Penelope said. "On my website, you know for references when producers and studios are looking to hire a caterer, it's good to have a history of higher profile jobs, and upcoming ones, so you appear well connected and active."

"What about this one, at the theater?" Doyle asked.

"No," Penelope said. "This is just a small project, a favor to the Madisons, really."

"So, maybe it's something to do with them," Doyle said.

"Maybe," Penelope said darkly. "I'd hate to think Elspeth wanted to run a con on Arlena or Randall and might have been trying to use me to do it."

"Would connect a few things," Doyle said, jotting down another note. "Less of a coincidence when you think about it. You're the common link between the theater and the Madison family, where they are working on a project."

"So," Penelope said, talking quicker. "Maybe her plan was if she didn't get on the Big Apple Dancing team, she'd try and get hired on as a chef for my crew."

"That's something that makes some kind of sense," Doyle said. "What do you think of that résumé that was attached to the letter?"

"It looks good," Penelope said. "The degree, some good experience listed. I would've been interested in this candidate."

"But you know now it's probably all made up," Doyle said.

"It can't all be made up, really," Penelope said. "Isn't there a saying about every falsehood contains a kernel of truth?"

"I'm not sure I've heard that one before," Doyle said doubtfully.

Penelope pulled out her phone and dialed the number of the first place on the résumé, a restaurant where Elspeth listed herself as a server several years earlier.

"Victory Diner," a man's voice shouted over the phone.

"Can I speak to the manager?" Penelope asked, then put the phone on speaker after the man who answered dropped the phone on something hard and walked away from the receiver. Penelope could hear him shouting in another language, his voice still strong in the distance. After a few minutes a woman picked up and barked out a hello.

"Hi, I'm checking a reference on an employee," Penelope said. "Elspeth Connor? She's listed that she worked at your restaurant back in 2012."

"Elspeth, right," the woman said hoarsely. "Yep. Good employee." Penelope could hear dishes clanging in the background and several different voices shouting.

Penelope looked at the phone number and the Seattle area code. "What kind of restaurant is it that you have there?" she asked.

"Greek," the woman said. "Will that be all? I got a line here."

"And you're in Seattle, Washington?"

"Duvall. Right outside," the woman said impatiently.

"Oh wait," Penelope said, "it looks like I got the date wrong. She was there in 2010, right?"

The woman hesitated a moment. "She was here for a while. Whatever she told you, that's the date. Look I gotta go." The woman hung up abruptly. Penelope stared at Doyle, who shrugged from his chair.

"Checks out," he said with a sigh.

"Um, no," Penelope said. "That woman didn't check any dates or files. I could've asked her to confirm anything."

"What are you saying?" Doyle asked.

"I'm saying either that woman doesn't confirm employment correctly for anyone, or there's a link to whoever Elspeth really is at a diner in Duvall, Washington."

"You might have something there," Doyle said. An appreciative look had overtaken his usual exhausted expression.

"Another thing. I don't usually get mailed letters and résumés. I mean sometimes, but normally it's emails." She set the resume and letter on his desk.

"I'll check the other places," Doyle said.

"Let me call the school," Penelope said, already pulling out her phone. "Looks like a community college or trade school maybe." She dialed the number and pressed the prompts to be connected to the records office. The recording said they were closed for the holiday but to leave a message and someone would call her back. Penelope left her number and hung up.

"Maybe I should just call them all," Penelope said, itching to call the next company down on the list.

"We'll get to that. Our victim might have wanted to mail it so her email couldn't be traced," Doyle said. "And if she was a con artist like we're thinking she might have been, she could've lined up references that would vouch for her."

"Wouldn't it be easier to create a fake email? Reroute her IP address, or something like that?"

Doyle dropped his pen on the pad and sat back. "Whatever this young woman was up to, I'm afraid it might have gotten her killed." The phone on his desk rang and he snatched it up. "Yeah?"

Penelope watched him listen to the voice on the other end. He began nodding and rubbed his mustache roughly with his fingers. "Okay, thanks."

"What is it?"

"The same weapon, a large serrated knife, was used in both murders," Doyle said. "The link between our two victims has been confirmed."

CHAPTER 36

"Let's go through it again, so I can take some notes," Doyle said.

Penelope described meeting Gabby at her local grocery market to Detective Doyle, who alternated between listening intently and raising a hand to slow her from time to time as he jotted down notes.

"And you were under the impression they were related," Detective Doyle said.

"Yes, I remember the younger woman referring to her as Mother, and they seemed close," Penelope said. "Although it didn't seem like there was a big enough age difference between them. I didn't realize it was a nickname."

"Well, you never know," Doyle said. "Some moms are younger when they have children."

"True," Penelope said.

"Had you ever seen them in that market before?" Doyle asked with a sigh.

"No," Penelope said. "But it was the day before Thanksgiving, and the place was packed with people I'd never seen before. Wait, what about the card they were trying to use?"

"I'm not sure that any information would have been captured by the store's register then, if the transaction didn't go through," Doyle said. "But I will ask them."

"They were walking," Penelope said. "I think they were headed to the bus stop on the main avenue that runs in front of the store. I thought about giving them a ride but..." Penelope trailed off, uncomfortable with how she thought about the women.

"You'd already done a good deed for the day," Doyle said. "It's not always a good idea to invite strangers into your car. It's better not to, actually."

"Still," Penelope said. "Maybe they were in Glendale visiting someone for the holiday."

"There's a train station there, right?" Doyle asked, rubbing his chin.

"Yes," Penelope said.

"So it would be easy enough for them to go back and forth between the city. Especially if they have family living by you."

"Right," Penelope said.

"I'll send your description to the shelters, see who Mother might have been traveling around with. Do you have time to look at some booking photos while you're here?"

"Sure," Penelope said. "If you think it will help."

"If we find out who the other woman is, that might lead us to who killed Mother. And possibly Elspeth," Doyle said, as he began tapping on his keyboard.

Penelope crossed her legs and leaned forward as the faces of different women filled the screen. After twenty minutes of looking into the eyes of a stream of middle-aged women who had been arrested in New York in the last few years, Penelope shook her head.

"I don't think I see her here," Penelope said. "Is this just New York?"

"Yeah, and just Manhattan," Doyle said.

"I have that New Jersey connection," Penelope said. "I can maybe look at some photos when I get home later."

"I appreciate your willingness to help," Doyle said, folding his hands together on his desk. "But I don't want you to get caught up in anything dangerous. You're not police."

"I know," Penelope said.

"I should let you get back. Thanks for the information you've provided."

CHAPTER 37

When Penelope returned to the theater, she found Francis outside in the truck, getting things prepped for dinner service.

"Hey, Boss," Francis said. "Miss Madison wanted me to let you know the crew is set up upstairs."

"Okay, thanks," Penelope said. She crossed the street and headed to the penthouse.

"There you are," Arlena said. "Everyone, this is Penelope, my right hand, and our head chef."

The dozen or so people in the room muttered hellos or waved. Penelope looked at each of them, then did a double take. "You hired an all female crew?"

Arlena smiled. "I sure did."

One of the women set down a shoulder cam on the large center meeting table and shook Penelope's hand.

"How is this...?" Penelope began, then decided against saying anything further.

"Possible? I had my choice of crew, as the director and co-producer," Arlena said. "And my choice was hire women first. Plus, these ladies were the most qualified applicants. It was an easy decision."

"I think it's awesome," Penelope said.

"Where were you, anyway?" Arlena asked. The head sound tech came over with a clipboard and waited for their conversation to be over before asking Arlena a question.

"I'll tell you later," Penelope said, with a wave of her hand.

Arlena gave her a wink and turned her attention to the crew

member.

Penelope stepped to the window and looked down at the theater and her food truck tucked in the alley.

"Oh, Pen," Arlena said to her back.

"Yeah?"

"I have a girl coming to interview to be my assistant," Arlena said.

"Assistant?"

"Yeah, Daddy suggested it," Arlena said with a slight roll of her eyes.

"I think he might be on to something," Penelope said.

"Yeah," Arlena said. "I want you to like her too, so let me know what you think."

"Okay," Penelope said. "Sounds good." She went back to looking out the window and her bird's eye view of the truck. Francis was outside, scribbling the dinner menu on the wipe-able white board they stored beneath the truck.

A man shuffled down the sidewalk dressed in ragged clothes and a dirty coat. His hair and beard were bushy and unwashed. Penelope watched him walk slowly toward the truck, then stop and watch Francis from behind. Penelope didn't think Francis could sense the man behind him, and she willed her sous chef silently to turn around and notice him.

The homeless looking man stepped into the alley and approached Francis from behind. Penelope's heart rate picked up and she put a palm on the thick glass of the window.

Just as the man was close enough to reach out and touch him, Francis's head snapped around and he stood up. Penelope watched the two men talk for a minute, and then Francis step onto the truck and returned a few seconds later with a sandwich wrapped in plastic. He handed it to the man, who waved his thanks and trundled away in the direction of the shelter.

"What's going on down there?" Arlena asked. She draped an arm around Penelope's shoulders.

"I'm a little jumpy," Penelope said. She told her about her visit to the police station, and about Gabby Bainbridge's death.

"Oh Pen, I'm so sorry," Arlena said. She hugged her tightly.

"Do you need me right now?" Penelope said, pulling away from her friend. The room behind them was buzzing with activity.

"No, we're good," Arlena said. "You want to go home?"

"No, I'm going to check on dinner service, keep moving forward, you know?"

"That's the Pen I know," Arlena said. "But if you're not up to it, please don't feel like you have to stay for the show."

"I'll be okay," Penelope said. "I'm going to take a walk, clear my head."

"Good idea," Arlena said.

CHAPTER 38

Penelope stepped quickly down the sidewalk. She'd left her messenger bag up in the film office, only tucking her phone in her coat pocket and her ID and some cash in her jeans. She slowed to a stop when she reached the front door of the homeless shelter on the next block. Faded flyers were taped to the glass door, little tags of paper with phone numbers fluttering in the breeze. One was giving information for an AA meeting nearby, and another was offering guitar lessons for twenty bucks an hour.

She paused for a second and thought about moving ahead with her walk. But something made her reach out and tug on the door.

Stepping inside the dim entryway, Penelope saw a woman at a desk to her left, and just beyond in the lobby, several people sat at tables watching a daytime talk show on the television.

"Help you?" the woman asked. She sat forward in her chair, her ill-fitting uniform shirt tugging at her shoulders.

"Hi," Penelope said. "I'm not sure if I'm in the right place, but I was wondering if you could tell me about one of your residents?"

Penelope watched the woman's guard go up, her expression hardening. "You police?" she asked.

"No," Penelope said quickly. "I'm a chef."

The woman let out a small laugh. "A chef, huh? We don't get too many of those in here. First time for everything, I guess."

Penelope leaned an elbow on the tall desk. "I'm Penelope. What's your name?"

"Brandi," the woman said. "With an I." Penelope wondered how many times Brandi had said that in her lifetime.

"The thing is, Brandi," Penelope began, "the day before Thanksgiving I met a couple of women who I think might stay here sometimes, at least one of them does. Did. We exchanged information. I was trying to track her down to follow up."

"How much she owe you?" Brandi said with a chuckle. Her hair had been braided close to her scalp in an intricate pattern of rows with strands of magenta and gold threaded through the strands. Her lipstick was a matching magenta shade and perfectly complimented her smooth brown skin.

"Oh, it's not a money thing," Penelope said. "It's actually..." Penelope stalled, trying to think of how to word her next statement. "I think she got mixed up with the wrong person somehow."

"You talking about Mother?" Brandi asked. "Cops already been in here asking about her."

"Yes. Gabby Bainbridge," Penelope said. "She had my card on her when..."

"When some monster killed her?" Brandi said matter-of-factly.

"Yes," Penelope said. They shared a moment of silence. "Why was she known as Mother, anyway?"

Brandi stood up so she and Penelope were eye to eye, with only the desk separating them. "That's what everyone called her. Because she was like a mother to the young ones, coming in fresh off the street. She said she was a nurse back in the day, midwife too, the way she told it. They've been calling her Mother for as far back as the beginning of time."

"Oh," Penelope said. A new wave of sadness washed over her. She remembered how full of life Gabby had seemed at the market, her mischievous grin and energetic personality. All of those things gone now, taken away by a killer.

"How long did Mother stay here?" Penelope asked.

Brandi shrugged again. "Mother has always been here. Way before I have, anyhow."

"Did she have a family?" Penelope asked. She looked over her shoulder at the common area and saw no one was paying attention to them, all eyes were focused on the television. A woman on the screen was yelling at a man who stared at the floor. The caption beneath them read *Paternity Test Reveals!*

"I think so," Brandi said. "But I'm not sure. She might have had children at some point, she said something about a man once. But no one came around here to see her, that's for sure."

"She ever say anything about New Jersey?"

Brandi shrugged and shook her head.

"If Mother had a family, why would she stay in a shelter?"

Brandi looked at her sadly. "It's not that simple. What did you say your name was again?"

"Sorry, it's Penelope," she mumbled.

"It's not that simple, Penelope," Brandi said. "I bet almost everyone in this place has some kind of kin somewhere. Family is complicated, they don't always want you around. Especially if you're struggling with...things."

"Was there anyone she hung around with? I saw her one time with a middle-aged lady over in Jersey."

"Hm," Brandi said, thinking. "She kind of hung around with everyone, you know? I don't remember her mentioning New Jersey. I'm going to tell you, because you seem like a nice person. This isn't a place people come to talk about things. We offer a clean bed and a hot meal, a place to rest for part of the day. We help folks get back on their feet, but we're not a hospital staffed with counselors."

One of the men in the other room got up from his chair and headed toward the desk. He wore a faded green jacket and black sweatpants and his hair was shot through with silver.

"Heading to the library," he said to Brandi. "You want me to bring you back a new book?"

Brandi picked up a library book from her desk and checked where her bookmark was, tucked near the end of a Sue Grafton novel, the title near the middle of the alphabet.

"Get me L if it's not checked out," Brandi said.

"You got it," he said. He bowed slightly at Penelope and her eyes fell to his jacket, where a row of small pins had been stuck through the rough fabric.

"Wait, sir?" Penelope asked after he turned to go. She dug in her coat pocket and found the little metal disk she'd tucked in there a few days earlier.

"Yeah, you want a book too? I charge a buck for each trip, bringing them to you or taking them back."

"No, I don't need a library book," Penelope said. Her fingers found the medal and she held it up to him. "Do you recognize this?"

The man looked at the medal in her palm and smiled. He plucked it carefully from her, his fingers stained yellow from what had to be years of smoking.

"That's a service medal," he said. He pointed to his own row of medals. "I got one too. Vietnam." He turned it over and looked at the back to reveal a dragon hidden behind a row of bamboo trees.

"Who would've gotten one like this?" Penelope asked.

"Anyone who spent more than a day in the jungle," the man said. "Long time ago now, before you were born. Like to see kids today try and defend this country like we did. Down in the marshes, not playing video games behind a screen."

"Okay, Bill," Brandi said with a smile. "Thanks for getting my book for me."

The man waved a hand and a smile came back to his face, the irritation slipping away. "You got it, Brandi. You know I didn't mean you. You're a hard worker, not like the rest of them."

After Bill left, Penelope said, "Thanks for your help, Brandi."

"Why you so interested in Mother, anyway? I didn't believe that story you told when you first got here, by the way. I'm young but I've been around the block a lot of times already."

Penelope laughed. "I can see that. Actually, I did meet Mother, and another woman she was with, where I live in New Jersey. We talked, and I liked her. When I heard what happened I just wanted to..."

"I know," Brandi said. She placed a cool palm on Penelope's hand. "It's a shock sometimes when people pass. It's good of you to check up on her." Brandi sat back in her chair, which groaned slightly under her weight. She bumped her mouse on the way down and her screen saver dissolved away, revealing a job search website.

"How long have you worked here?" Penelope asked.

Brandi sighed and rubbed her chin. "My uncle got me the job about a year ago, right after I finished up community college. I work for the city for a while, they pay off half my student loans."

"What did you go to school for, if you don't mind my asking?" Penelope asked.

"Business administration," Brandi said. "My year in here is almost up," she said, pointing a close-cropped magenta fingernail at the screen. "I got my eye on a couple of things, planning to make a move. I like helping the people here, don't get me wrong. But it's not a salary I can live with long term, know what I mean? Not in this city."

"I do," Penelope said. "Well, thank you for all your help, Brandi."

"You're welcome," Brandi said.

"Oh, if you want to stop down for lunch one day, that's my food truck outside the Vitrine," Penelope said. "If I'm not there tell the guys I sent you."

Brandi smiled. "I bet a lot of people try and say the chef said it was okay to grab a free lunch." She laughed and rocked back and forth in her chair.

"Okay, I'll give you a password you can use, then they'll know it's been cleared."

"Hmm," Brandi said. "That might work."

"Pickles," Penelope said. "Say 'pickles' and lunch is on me. As a thanks. Also, here's my card. If you think of anything else about Mother, give me a ring, okay?"

"Sure," Brandi said. "And thanks for the lunch offer. You're all right."

CHAPTER 39

"Bainbridge?" Arlena asked. "Why is that familiar?"

The room around them was buzzing with activity. The crew had set up different stations with video monitors and computers. One of the bedrooms was a storage area for cameras, lights and microphones. A large white board had been propped up against the wall on the left next to the fireplace. Arlena had been tacking index cards to it in different colors, creating a storyboard for them all to work from.

Some of the cards referenced Ruby, some had notes about a few of the current dancers. And one sat off by itself with Elspeth's name scrawled on it with a question mark below it.

"Bainbridge is the name of the ghost that haunts the Vitrine," Penelope said.

"How poetic," Arlena said. "She took the name of a ghost."

"Or that's her real name," Penelope said. "Isn't that weird?"

"Well, it's not that uncommon of a name," Arlena hedged.

"I guess," Penelope said, unconvinced.

The door to the suite opened and Max sauntered in. He eyed the activity in the room with an approving glance.

"Well, look who it is," Arlena said. She set down the note cards and put her hands on her hips.

"How did you get up here? Daddy said I was giving you a key. Did you get one from him?"

"No," Max said. "I buzzed a few apartments until someone let me in."

Penelope's heart sank at his words and she made a note to

bring this up to Armand and Martha. It was common for people to accidentally buzz the wrong people into apartment buildings, thinking they are doing their neighbors a favor or allowing in a delivery, but it was definitely not the safest practice.

"Please thank your friend Ashley for announcing my engagement for me," Arlena said. "I hope he got a nice payday out of it."

Penelope took a step backwards, hoping to stay out of the brother-sister argument.

"Whoa," Max said with a laugh. "Ashley wouldn't do that."

"How do you know?" Arlena asked. "How well do you know him anyway?"

"I know him well enough to know he wouldn't betray a trust like that," Max said.

Arlena looked at him doubtfully. "Max, you gain and shed friends faster than most people do their socks."

"You know what? Let's ask him."

Arlena rolled her eyes and turned away from him. "Whatever. Like he's going to tell you the truth now."

Max stared at her as he pulled out his phone. He gazed down and sent a text. "I'll clear this up. And who cares anyway, aren't you happy everyone knows?"

"Yes," Arlena said. "No. I wanted to have it be special. To come from us."

"It's still special," Penelope said. "The fact that you're committing to each other."

"Yeah, I know," Arlena said, relenting. "I for once want things to go as I plan them, that's all."

Max's phone buzzed in his hand. He read the screen and turned it around to show Arlena the words: *NO WAY! WASN'T ME, BRO!*

"See?" Max said. "I told you."

"Well, that's all the evidence I need," Arlena said flatly. "Bro."

CHAPTER 40

Penelope stepped onto her kitchen truck after sliding the side door open. She decided to leave the sparring Madison siblings on their own.

"How's it going in here?" Penelope asked.

Francis turned to her from the grill and smiled. "All good in the neighborhood."

He flipped over a row of chicken breasts with one smooth motion, then picked up a sauté pan and flicked his wrist, sending a wave of mushrooms into the air.

"How you doing?" he asked.

Alex, one of her other chefs stuck his head in the service window. "Hey, Boss. We're all set up inside."

"Okay," Penelope said. She opened a small closet right behind the front driver section and pulled out a chef coat with Red Carpet Catering stitched across one side and her name right below it.

She and her two chefs transported hotel pans full of food through the back door of the theater and up a few wooden stairs to the dressing room hallway and through to the break room.

Alex had already set up the serving tray holders and lit the burners beneath to warm the water the food pans would sit in. Delicious smells of grilled chicken and salmon filled the small space. Penelope eyed the tray of ice on the counter next to the sink where they would have their salad bar with three different kinds of lettuce and a variety of toppings.

After a few more trips to the truck and the table outside behind it, they'd moved all of the food inside. Penelope reached under the tablecloth and pulled out a bag full of disposable dinner plates and another filled with cutlery. She set them out on the last table closest to the door, so the crew and dancers would be able to grab them first before going through the line they'd created to grab dinner.

"Smells wonderful," Armand said.

"Oh, great," Penelope said with a smile. She straightened her chef coat and brushed the edge of the tablecloth. "I hope everyone will enjoy it."

"Oh my dear, I'm certain they will," Armand said, peeking under the foil covering the nearest steam table. "I think Arlena is filming tonight's show. Well, not Arlena herself, you know, the crew."

"Do you normally record any of the shows?" Penelope asked.

"We do one or two each year for the archives," Armand said, his eyes rolling over the salad station. "And news crews come sometimes to film a few scenes to go along with their coverage of the theater, or Broadway in general."

"How long have you been doing that?" Penelope asked.

"As long as I can remember," Armand said. "I'd have to check and see how old the tapes go back. And you know, video disintegrates, so..."

"Right," Penelope said. "I was thinking maybe you'd have footage of Ruby for Arlena."

"Quite possible," Armand said. He rubbed his palms together. "Shall I ring the dinner bell then?"

Penelope laughed, picturing Armand in his elegant suit on a country porch ringing a bell. "Yes, let's let them through."

CHAPTER 41

Penelope watched the dancers file through the room, helping a few of them here, grabbing bottles of water or tea, and explaining what a few of the items were on hand.

After everyone had been served, Penelope wandered through the dressing room area, where a few of the dancers had decided to eat, propping their plates on makeup desks and chatting with each other. Out on the stage, Penelope saw a group of them sitting in a circle, plates on their laps, eating quietly together.

Abigail sat off by herself in the corner, her knees pulled up, her plate on the floor next to her. She picked at some lettuce, and her chicken breast was untouched.

"Hey," Penelope said. "You don't like your dinner?"

"No," Abigail sighed. "It tastes great. And it's free. Nothing tastes better than free food."

"I'm glad you like it," Penelope said. She crouched down next to Abigail and put a hand on her shoulder. "What's going on?"

Abigail pulled her phone from her sweatshirt pocket, swiped it to life and held it out for Penelope to see.

"I just got this," Abigail said.

Penelope squinted at the screen. She recognized a small print hanging near the kitchen area of a set of ballet shoes. "Is that your apartment?"

"Yes," Abigail said. "Look closer."

Penelope enlarged the photo and saw the top of a woman's head, appearing to be asleep in bed, a few dark red curls snaking out over the comforter.

"Is that...Elspeth?" Penelope asked.

"Yeah," Abigail said. "Asleep in her bed. Who could've taken this picture?"

"And why are they sending it to you now?" Penelope asked.

Abigail shrugged. "It came from one of those anonymous apps that hides the identity of the sender."

"I didn't know that was a thing," Penelope admitted. While she was only in her late twenties, Penelope sometimes felt ancient around women Abigail's age, even though she couldn't even be ten years younger.

"Yeah, Pinger, TextFree. Those are a few of them," Abigail said.

"For what purpose?" Penelope asked, not sure she wanted to know the answer.

"It's for trolls, mostly," Abigail said. "So they can leave anonymous comments online, or keep their identity a secret while communicating."

"Sounds like it could be dangerous," Penelope said. "What's to stop a stalker from targeting unsuspecting women? Luring them into something dangerous?"

"It's not a safe world out there," Abigail said. "Should I be freaked out about this? I feel like I should be."

Abigail sat down on the stage and crossed her legs, staring at the photo.

"This was taken before she died, right?" Penelope asked.

"I guess," Abigail said. "But why send it to me?"

"I'm not sure," Penelope said. "But I think we should tell Detective Doyle about it."

"Okay," Abigail said. She tucked her hands inside her sweatshirt sleeves and curled in further on herself.

CHAPTER 42

Penelope hung up with Detective Doyle after explaining what she'd seen on Abigail's phone, then went back to the break room to help Francis and Alex clean up, cover and store the leftovers.

"Not many opted for the grilled steak," Penelope said, eyeing the hotel pan halfway full of medium rare beef.

"We can make something else with it for tomorrow. Steak and eggs for breakfast?" Alex said.

"Good idea," Penelope said.

They took most of the pans and slid them into the refrigerator in the break room, then stowed away the plates and cups, leaving a few out for any stragglers.

"Good service," Penelope said.

A young man entered the break room, pulling off his jacket. "Did I miss dinner? I had a doctor's appointment."

Penelope recognized the man from the orchestra pit as one of the musicians. "There's still plenty, go ahead."

They watched him help himself to a salad and some chicken then take a seat at the table they'd just cleared away.

"Thanks," he said between hurried mouthfuls. "It's a long night without some food in my stomach."

"You guys are doing two shows, right?" Penelope asked.

"Yeah, the doubles are a killer," he said, chewing a piece of lettuce.

"Hey, weren't you the one who heard Elspeth Connor say she was from Phoenix?" Penelope asked.

The musician slowed his chewing and eyed her carefully.

"Yeah, I'm pretty sure she said she was. It was this one time when we were outside waiting to be let in."

"Did she say where in Phoenix?" Penelope asked.

"No, but it was weird because she said it was colder than Phoenix that day," he said. "I think she was trying to be funny but it didn't make sense. When is Phoenix cold?"

Penelope's phone buzzed in her pocket and she pulled it out. Seeing Joey's name she smiled and excused herself, ducking backstage behind the curtains.

"Thought I'd catch you before show time," Joey said. "Is now good?"

"Yes," Penelope said. "What are you up to?"

"Got a little shopping done," Joey said. "A few names have been crossed off my list."

"Oh yeah?" Penelope asked. "Like who?"

"Like Ma, and I got my dad a new fishing pole," Joey said, his tone playful.

"What did you get for your new partner? You guys doing a secret Santa at the station?"

"Ha," Joey said. "Clarissa...I'll probably get her a gift card. What do you get for the woman who wants nothing from anyone?"

"Give her a break," Penelope said. "She puts up with you all day. That deserves a little something at least."

"You're teasing me again," Joey said. "Hey, when are you coming home?"

"Well, the first show starts in twenty, and they're doing a double feature tonight. But dinner is finished, so we can probably clear down and get out of here soon."

"Good," Joey said. "I miss you."

"I'll probably hop on the train," Penelope said. "Arlena's going to work late tonight, but It's been a long day."

"Okay, see you soon then?"

"Yean, also...I was wondering if you could show me some mug shots? A woman I met in the grocery might be tied into what happened to the murdered dancer."

"Okay," Joey said, a note of hesitation in his voice. "I suppose I could do that. Text me the particulars and I'll load the iPad. And let me know when you're close to leaving."

"I will," Penelope said. "Thanks. Love you."

The curtain next to her rustled and she glanced at it. She knew she hadn't brushed it or bumped it, and figured it was a random breeze, probably from someone opening the back door. She kept quiet for a minute, then stepped around, holding her breath to be as silent as possible.

Creeping around the heavy curtain, she jumped when the orchestra began practicing, then continued to the main backstage area. Looking up, she saw Armand on his office's balcony, looking down at the stage and the dancers who were getting assembled.

"Armand," Penelope called up to him.

He cupped a hand behind his ear and leaned over farther.

"Who was just here?" she called.

Armand shook his head and shrugged, holding his hands up in the air. He pointed to the orchestra, indicating to her he couldn't hear her over the music.

Penelope shouted then. "Who was just here? Backstage?"

Armand stared at her in confusion and then mouthed something in return. The music got louder and Penelope froze when she saw a figure move out on the balcony behind Armand.

"Turn around!" Penelope shouted.

Armand continued to mouth wordlessly at her, pointing to the orchestra on stage.

Penelope waved her hands in the air, willing him to turn around. The person edged closer to Armand on the balcony and Penelope tried to make out their face. The person was short, and cloaked in a large coat with a large hood that obscured the face, but a wiry beard stuck out from the bottom. Penelope saw black gloves on the person's hands, as they reached out toward Armand.

"Stop!" Penelope yelled.

At the last second, Armand turned halfway around, just as the person behind him shoved him over the balcony.

CHAPTER 43

"Hang on!" Penelope called up to Armand, who had grabbed onto one of the balcony railings with his hands.

Penelope rushed out to the stage from behind the curtain and yelled at the conductor. "Help me!"

The man froze and stared at her, then waved his baton in the air to stop the music.

"What on earth?" he asked.

"It's Armand! He's going to fall!"

With that she turned and ran toward the stairway that led up to his office. The conductor and a few musicians scrambled out of the pit and followed her.

Armand clung onto the railing, his shoulders rigid and his legs cycling through the air. The person who had shoved him was gone, vanished back inside the office.

"We're coming!" Penelope said. "Hold on!"

Penelope took two steps at a time up the rickety wooden staircase, not feeling her legs beneath her, adrenaline coursing through her veins. The orchestra members followed her up the stairs that rattled beneath her feet, and she wondered how long ago they'd been built and if they'd hold up for at least one more day.

The conductor stood below, barking orders to the remaining musicians, telling some to head in one direction and the others on the opposite side. A few of the dancers had emerged from the dressing rooms, partially made up and a few already dressed in their costumes for the show.

"What's happening?" one of them cried.

Penelope reached the office suite and banged through the door, moving quickly through the outer to the inner office and out onto the balcony. She fell down on her knees and poked her hands through the wood slats, grabbing onto Armand's wrists.

"You've come for me," Armand panted. Penelope could smell a slight whiff of alcohol on his breath. Faint, but still there, as if he'd had a glass of wine with dinner.

"Hang on," Penelope said.

The two musicians who had followed her leaned over on either side of her to grab onto Armand.

Penelope could feel his hands were slick with sweat and she grabbed onto his wrists harder as he slid further down the slats.

"Don't let go, dear," Armand said.

"We've got you," Penelope said.

The conductor had grabbed a spare curtain from backstage and the musicians had it stretched out below Armand. Penelope wondered how strong the fabric was, and how strong the musicians holding it were. A man, however slender and lithe as Armand was, would still be hard to catch in a fall with momentum gathering on the way down.

"I've got him," the musician on her left shouted. "Grab onto me so I don't go over with him," he hissed with effort as he grasped Armand's wrists.

Penelope was reluctant to let go, but stood up quickly, moving behind the man to help anchor him on the right side of the balcony.

The other musician kept his grip on Armand's wrist and they both began to pull.

"Swing yourself up," one of them said.

Armand almost chuckled. "I'm afraid those days are behind me, my boy."

"You can do it," Penelope said.

Armand smiled sadly and let loose his grip. The musicians pulled him harder, trying to get the dead weight of the man up and over to safety.

One last heave and his torso appeared above the railing.

Armand seemed to return to them, hoisting himself forward and back onto the balcony, his long legs flopping over inelegantly at the end.

He lay in a tangle of arms and legs on the floor, his chest heaving and his face red and sweating.

"Thank goodness," Penelope said. She began to shake as the adrenaline worked its way through her system. "I saw them. I saw who pushed you."

"Bainbridge again," Armand said.

"It was no ghost this time," Penelope said. "Whoever it was, they were real."

CHAPTER 44

"Looks like they went out through here," Detective Doyle said, leaning out an open window in the back room of the office suite. "You're going to have to keep these locked from now on, Mr. Wagner."

Armand sat on the sofa in his office and nodded through the open doorway at the detective. Penelope sat next to him and felt the tremors that still rustled through his body from the shock of being dangled over the balcony.

"I might have been killed, you know," he said to Doyle. "You must find out who is doing this to my theater. Who is out to hurt us?"

"We need your help to figure it out, Mr. Wagner," Doyle said. "Did you recognize your assailant?"

"No," Armand said. "I only caught a glimpse, to be honest. I was mainly focusing on not falling to my death."

Doyle nodded. "I know. But is there anything that you can think of? Any distinguishing features?"

"All I know is one of the bums from down the street has taken aim at the Vitrine, for some reason probably known only to him. And he's making our lives hell, through no fault of our own."

"Okay," Doyle said with a sigh. He looked through a few items on Armand's desk then headed for the door. He turned at the last minute. "You, Miss Sutherland, I might need to put a protective detail on you."

"No, you don't. I am being careful. I was going to take the train home tonight but Arlena insists I take a car."

"There was one odd thing, Detective," Armand said suddenly. He stared off in space as if in a trance.

"What's that?" Doyle said.

"The smell was missing," Armand said.

"Excuse me? What smell?" Doyle pressed him.

"The odor, the decay smell, that comes from people living on the street," Armand said with a shrug. "The person who pushed me smelled like..."

Doyle leaned forward, willing Armand to speak more quickly. "Like what?"

"Like roses," Armand said simply. "Quite beautiful roses."

CHAPTER 45

Joey opened the door of his apartment and Penelope hurried inside, falling into his arms.

"I've missed you," Penelope said.

"Hey," Joey chuckled. "You too, but it's only been a day or two, right?"

Penelope hugged him harder. "I know but it feels like forever this time."

Joey led her through to the living room where he had a bottle of wine open on the table and two glasses set out. Penelope pulled off her coat and hung it across one of the stools that anchored the island on the far end near the kitchen and eased down onto Joey's leather sofa.

He poured her a glass of wine and she eagerly took a sip.

"Did you get those photos?" Penelope asked.

"My day was fine, thank you," Joey teased.

"Sorry," Penelope said. She tapped her fingers on her knee and said, "How was your day?"

"Fine," Joey said. He kissed her on the cheek and reached over to his iPad which was on the coffee table. "And I got your photos. Hopefully, anyway."

Penelope scrolled through the pictures of the women. Looking at their faces was very much the same as looking at the ones in Doyle's office. She could see that some of them were having the worst day of their lives at the moment the photo had been taken, while some looked confused, or out of it, and some appeared amused by the whole situation.

"There!" Penelope said. "That's her!" She tilted the screen toward Joey and he squinted at the information below it.

"Helen Chadwick," Joey said. "Burglary, petit theft, prostitution. She's been a busy lady the past thirty years."

Penelope looked into the woman's eyes, a mischievous glint staring back at her from the photo. Her face appeared puffy and well worn, sun damage dotting her forehead and cheeks, and blotching the puffiness around her eyes.

"What's that say?" Penelope asked, pointing to the final list of charges beneath Helen's photo.

"Fraud," Joey said.

Penelope sat back against the couch.

Joey tapped a few things on the iPad. "Check fraud, looks like. Credit cards too. She was caught using her neighbor's identity to open several accounts, then she wrote a series of bad checks."

"Where in New Jersey?" Penelope asked.

Joey tapped his chin with a finger as he read from the screen. "That incident wasn't here. The shoplifting and prostitution happened here. The fraud was years ago, looks like upstate New York somewhere. Why is this person of interest to you?" Joey asked, setting down the iPad on the table and moving closer to Penelope.

"I paid for some groceries for her and who I thought was her mother the day before Thanksgiving," Penelope said. "And now that woman has been killed, maybe by the same person who killed the dancer. She had my card on her when she died."

Joey sat up straighter. He reached out and gently pulled Penelope's chin around with his finger, so they were eye to eye. "Do not get involved with this woman. She's a criminal, you don't know how people like this will react when confronted."

Penelope's gaze fell to his chin. "I know."

"Please," Joey said. "Promise me."

Penelope looked him in the eyes. "I promise. I don't want anything to happen to me either."

CHAPTER 46

The next morning Penelope rode into the city on the train. She popped her earbuds in and listened to a local news broadcast but kept the volume low and did not let herself become distracted by anything around her. She kept an eye on the people sitting nearby, in an effort to be vigilant like Joey had drilled into her that morning over breakfast at his apartment.

She checked her text messages again. She hadn't heard back from Detective Doyle after she sent Helen Chadwick's name to him before she fell asleep at Joey's. While she promised Joey she would be careful, she was still going to try and find out where the real Elspeth had disappeared to, and what connection Helen might have to the case, if any. All very carefully, of course.

"Always know who's behind you," Joey had said over coffee in his kitchen that morning. "Cross the street if the same person has followed you for more than two blocks. Hop in a cab the minute you feel off about anyone around."

"I've got my street smarts," Penelope said. "I can handle myself."

"I don't like your name coming up in connection with a killer, or this fraud woman," Joey said. "I know you can handle yourself, but being extra careful is important right now."

The train shot into the tunnel and the conductor came through, swaying in the aisle to check the final tickets before arrival. He stopped at a group of girls and waited as they each flashed a pass at him. Penelope caught the last one that was imprinted with the word "Student" in bright blue letters. The conductor tipped his hat at Penelope as he passed.

Penelope began to gather her things, slipping her earbuds out and tugging her phone from her pocket.

On the screen was a text with a tiny picture attached. Penelope squinted and pulled it open just as the brakes squealed against the tracks and the car jarred quickly from left to right as it made a slight turn. Penelope tapped on the text and enlarged the picture. At first she couldn't tell what she was looking at. Then her eyes widened and she gripped the phone tighter as she gazed at the image.

It was Abigail, her wrists bound and her mouth taped shut, her eyes closed and her head lolling over to one side.

"Wait," Penelope said, as the picture began to dissolve and fade away. She focused on Abigail's face and on the clothes she was wearing. It looked like the same sweatshirt and tank top she'd seen her in yesterday, but she couldn't tell if the color was right because the picture was pixelating and disappearing right in front of her eyes.

Penelope stood up from her seat before the train came to a stop, then bolted from the car the minute the doors opened. She jogged up the stairs from the platform, jostling aside slower moving commuters as she took the steps two at a time.

When she reached the main terminal of Penn Station, she paused near a wide round pillar and looked at her phone again. The picture was gone, but there was a message in its place. It read *Hurry Up or # 3 is on U. 5K or she dies.*

With shaking hands Penelope dialed Detective Doyle's number and pressed the phone to her ear.

"Yeah?" Doyle answered in his sleepy voice.

"Someone's got Abigail!"

CHAPTER 47

Penelope took a cab uptown, willing the driver to move faster, scanning the faces of the people on the sidewalk as they went. She knew this was a useless activity, in a city with more than eight million people, the chances were zero she'd come across the one person she desperately wanted to find. But there was nothing else to do on the ride, and it kept her from jumping out at every red light and making a run for the Theater District.

When they finally pulled up in front of the Vitrine, she leapt from the cab and sprinted to the apartment building, fumbled her key into the lock and slapped the elevator button. Pressing the button for twelve, she focused on her breath, willing herself to not panic. She pictured Abigail safe in her apartment, free from harm, hoping against hope the girl was fine and this was all a hoax, another cruel prank.

Penelope hurried down the hallway to Abigail's apartment, her heart sinking when she saw the door was slightly ajar, the deadbolt keeping it from closing all the way. She tented her fingers and pushed it open slowly, peering inside as much as the space would allow, ready to duck back in the hallway quickly if she came upon anyone besides Abigail inside.

The elevator pinged in the hallway behind her as she opened the door the whole way.

It was empty, no sign of Abigail in the tiny studio.

"Step back," Doyle said behind her. "Wait out in the hallway, Penelope."

"She's gone," Penelope said.

Doyle gave her a sympathetic glance then stepped inside, a uniformed officer he'd brought with him following closely behind.

"Looks like struggle happened here," Doyle said.

Penelope saw the piles of clothes strewn around the room and the unmade beds he was looking at. "I think that's how she kept the place, actually."

Doyle nodded slightly and pointed to a chair near the window that was overturned. "That's something maybe."

Penelope's heart sank as she stared at the chair. "Maybe you're right."

Doyle looked in the sink and pulled open the refrigerator, his eyes roving over the takeout cartons and a bottle of vodka chilling in the freezer. "Not a health nut, I see."

"Detective," Penelope said. "Someone is holding her captive. We have to find her."

"Get a team down here," he said to the uniformed officer. "Let's look for prints, question the rest of the girls on the floor."

The officer nodded sharply and stepped past Penelope out into the hallway, pulling his phone out to make a call.

"This one isn't like the others then," Doyle said. "If there's a connection. We haven't seen a photograph of the victim before the...end. Actually I still haven't seen the photo." He gave Penelope a stern glance.

"It disappeared," Penelope said. "I swear I saw her."

Doyle raised his hand and showed her his palm. "I believe you. I just don't know what this guy is after. Killing a dancer, killing an older homeless woman, kidnapping another dancer, the friend of the murdered girl. Do you see what I'm getting at here?"

"They don't match each other," Penelope said. "But they're related. Abigail and Elspeth through their friendship."

"And Gabby Bainbridge through the weapon," Doyle said.

"And Bainbridge connects the theater too," Penelope added.

"One big puzzle with too many clues to make any sense. It doesn't fit."

"Don't forget the attack on Armand," Penelope said. "Another box ticked for the theater."

Doyle put his hands on his hips and looked around the apartment. "The last thing I want is another dead girl on my watch."

CHAPTER 48

Penelope headed up to the suite and let herself in. Several of the crew members had arrived already and were working quietly either at the table or in the kitchen nook.

Her phone buzzed in her back pocket and she pulled it out quickly, staring at an unfamiliar number. She stepped into the empty bedroom suite and answered.

"Hello?" she said cautiously.

"Hello, this is John from Archer Academy returning your call," a man's voice said.

"Where?"

"Archer? You left a message inquiring about a reference from one of our students?"

"Oh, right," Penelope said, remembering Elspeth's résumé.

"I'm sorry to say we don't have a student registered by the name of Elspeth Connor, so we can't confirm the reference."

"That's strange," Penelope said. "It was listed on her CV, the one she used to apply for work."

"It's not that strange," the man said knowingly. "I get one or two a month, people listing academic credentials they don't quite have."

"But it's so easy to check that," Penelope said.

"And still a lot of employers don't bother," the man said. "Have a nice day."

"Wait," Penelope said. "Would you be able to check another name for me?"

"I can confirm if they have been a student here," the man said.

"I can't share other information besides that confirmation and the years of attendance."

"Okay," Penelope said, thinking. "I have a couple of other résumés here. Any students named Bainbridge? In the past ten years or so?"

"First name?" the man asked.

"Gabrielle," Penelope said, knowing Gabby would be too old, but thinking she should say something. She spelled the last name for him and listened to keys clicking on the other end of the line.

"Sorry, no Bainbridges in the past ten years," the man said. "You got another fraudulent résumé."

"Fraud," Penelope murmured, then quickly said, "I have one more name for you to check."

"Go ahead," the man said, amusement in his voice.

"Chadwick," Penelope said. "Helen Chadwick."

The typing continued and then a pause. "I have a Cassie Chadwick, confirmed as a student, however she did not complete the program here."

"Cassie Chadwick," Penelope said. "Was she a culinary student?"

"No, she was enrolled in beginning dance, but she dropped out after one term. Two years ago."

"And are you a community college?" Penelope asked.

"We're a trade school, but we have academic courses too, much like a community college, and we're accredited with the New York University system. We're the largest trade school in the area," he said.

"Where exactly are you located?" Penelope asked.

"Upstate," the man said. "Just north of Syracuse."

CHAPTER 49

Arlena came out of the bedroom and stretched her arms over her head just as Penelope hung up the phone and came out into the main part of the suite. She'd left a message for Doyle about Cassie Chadwick.

Arlena had on jeans and a sweater, and her long black hair was tousled from sleep.

"Did you spend the night?" Penelope asked.

"Yes," Arlena said with a yawn. "I was watching the dailies and then the editing team taught me how to use their equipment. We cut a few scenes from the show last night."

"The show must go on," Penelope said. "Even after the artistic director gets flung over a balcony."

"Hey," Arlena said, concern creasing her sleepy face. "What's up?"

Penelope explained about the picture she'd seen of Abigail. The woman in the kitchenette glanced up from her notes and eyed Penelope curiously.

"Did you happen to hear anything last night?" Penelope asked.

"No," Arlena said. "I'm sorry. We were working and then I conked out for a few hours."

"We need to keep the doors locked all the time up here," Penelope said to the room. Everyone nodded, then went back to their tasks.

A knock on the door made Penelope jump, and Arlena placed a hand on her shoulder. "Take a seat, relax for a bit. Or better yet, why don't you lie down for a while in the bedroom."

"I don't think I can rest," Penelope said. "I'm too worried about Abigail."

Arlena went to the door and opened it after a peek through the peephole, and Penelope went to the kitchen to pour a cup of coffee.

"Come in," Arlena said.

Penelope did a double take when she saw the young woman in the doorway.

"We can sit over here, have our interview," Arlena said. "Pen, this is..."

"Chamay," Penelope said. "From Steiners. The elf in the coffee shop."

"That's right," Chamay said with a laugh. "I thought you were going to say the elf on the shelf for a minute."

Chamay had changed out of her elf outfit and into a pair of black jeans, sneakers and a tight pink sweater. "I've applied to be Arlena's assistant."

"How did you know she needed an assistant?" Penelope asked.

"I saw an announcement through the agency I'm signed up with for temp to permanent work," Chamay said.

"You advertised you were looking for an assistant?" Penelope asked Arlena.

"Not exactly an advertisement. It's a private agency," Chamay said. "We register and have to be accepted to get the notices. The agency does background checks, things like that. I have as one of my preferences to work as an assistant, in a significant position, for a significant boss."

"Thanks for responding to the request," Arlena said.

Penelope set her coffee mug down on the counter. "I think I will rest for a minute."

"Yeah," Arlena said. "You've had a shock."

Penelope walked quickly into the bedroom and sat at the edge of the bed, her forearms on her thighs and her hands dangling between her legs. A row of file boxes had been stacked up against the back wall. Some numbers and what looked like years scrawled in magic marker on the side. Penelope lifted the lid on the closest one and saw a stack of photos and a few reels of tape. She went back to the bed and laid back, closing her eyes for a moment to try and sort through all of the information she had in her mind, piecing the elements of everything she knew together.

After a few minutes she heard a sharp laugh from the other side of the door and voices raised in jovial conversation. She felt like she was on another planet, one filled with angst and worry. What was happening to Abigail right now? Was she okay, or was she going to end up stuffed in some kind of case and dumped in an alley somewhere in the city? And where would it be this time? And how could she stop it?

CHAPTER 50

Penelope sat up in bed and was disoriented for a moment, then remembered she was in the suite in the apartment building.

"Abigail," she said, snatching her phone from the comforter next to her. The phone buzzed again, and she could see that it was the second notification and that she'd probably been roused from her doze by the first.

Another image appeared in thumbnail from an unknown number, and Penelope opened it. This time she immediately took a screenshot of the picture before it started pixelating away. It was Abigail again, her eyes open wide in fear. Her mouth was still taped, but it looked like more had been added. And to Penelope's dismay, a bruise had formed around one of her eyes, and her left cheek was red as if it had been struck.

Penelope took another screen shot, trying to see anything in the background of the picture that might give her an indication of where Abigail was being held.

The photo was gone and the message appeared: *# 3 Is Running Out of Time. 5K or she dies.*

Penelope forwarded the message and the screenshot of the picture to Detective Doyle, then awaited his response. After a moment of silence Penelope heard the outer door of the suite open and familiar voices fill the room on the other side of the bedroom door. She heard Max for sure, and Randall too.

Stepping into the suite, she saw both of them, and Sybil, Jackson and Dakota too. The little girl was dressed in a green coat with red tights and shiny Mary Janes. Jackson was standing behind one of the crew, watching the monitor as the editor worked on cutting some film.

"Daddy," Arlena said. "I didn't know the kids were coming up."

"We're taking them to the matinee," Randall said, eyeing the crew at work and nodding approvingly. "They've never seen the Christmas Extravaganza. It will be a treat for all of us. But first, here are some notes I made from reading Ruby's diary. I finally finished last night."

"What did you find out?" Arlena asked.

"I think from what I have put together, my mother was involved with a building developer turned politician. A guy named Aaron Beckwith."

"As in the Beckwith Group? The company that owns the theater?" Arlena asked.

"That's the one."

"Okay, I'll read through all of this later, see what narrative thread it fits the best with, if it does at all. Thanks, Daddy." She set the notes down on the table.

"I'm here to help too, with the production, whatever you need," Max said to Arlena.

"What happened to you?" Randall asked, eyeing Penelope in the doorway. "You look like you've seen a ghost."

"I hope not," Penelope said. "I got another picture of Abigail. I've sent it to the police."

"What is happening?" Sybil asked, keeping her eye on Dakota, who had begun to twirl in place in front of Penelope.

"It's..." Penelope began. "It's not something..."

"I've hired an assistant," Arlena said. "Penelope's got so much to deal with like you said, Daddy. Like this current situation. I can't rely on her for everything."

"Great news," Randall said.

"You hired Chamay?" Penelope asked.

"Yes!" Arlena said. "She's enthusiastic and knows a lot about me and my work already."

"Okay," Penelope said. "You don't want to consider any other candidates first?"

"I want to move on it," Arlena said. "I'm too busy right now anyway. That reminds me, can you get her situated with the accountant for payroll? You know what forms to fill out, since you do it for your chefs all the time."

"Sure," Penelope said with uncertainty. "Have her swing by the truck whenever. I keep that kind of stuff up front in my mobile office."

Max took a seat at the table and began leafing through a stack of papers, the day's call sheet and rough out of the scenes Arlena was hoping to get during the day.

"What should I do today? I don't see my name on the call sheet," Max said.

"I didn't know you were coming," Arlena said. "You know what would be great? We have to get started on the background research, pulling together an interesting narrative from the archives. The theater sent over the boxes yesterday. They're in the bedroom."

"Research?" Max asked. "I thought I'd be assistant director today."

"I could really use the help here," Arlena said. "It would be excellent to combine the historic photos, show the similarities between the performers of today with the ones from the past."

"Max, you should help Arlena how she wants you to help," Randall said. "She's in charge for a reason."

"Okay," Max said with a smile. "I can do anything. You know that."

"Perfect," Arlena said.

"I'm heading down, if anyone wants to join me," Penelope said. "We're doing an early supper later for anyone who is sticking around before the nighttime shows." Her phone buzzed in her pocket and she pulled it out, seeing a response from Doyle, and another text from an unknown number that read: *This is Brandi. I have something for you.*

CHAPTER 51

The matinee theater patrons had already begun to line up outside the Vitrine, eager looking tourists and families gazing up at the old building in anticipation of the spectacle they'd soon be seeing. Penelope led Randall and Sybil and the kids around to the back door and used her key to show them inside.

"I can't believe my mother used to work here," Randall said. "It's like I'm stepping back in time."

When they came out from backstage, Armand rushed over and grasped Randall's hands in his. "Mr. Madison, it's an honor to have you today."

A few of the dancers hurried past them, heading over to Martha, who stood at the front of the stage, talking to the orchestra conductor. She turned and gave them stern looks when they both started speaking at once with questions about the choreography.

"You should know this by now," Martha said in a low voice. "Just do it as we rehearsed."

"You'll be sitting in the front row, of course," Armand said. He bent at the waist and eyed Jackson and Dakota. "You're not going to believe your eyes, little ones."

Jackson looked slightly bored, but Dakota was bursting with excitement.

"I'll be outside with my team," Penelope said, leaving the group on the stage.

Detective Doyle was standing outside her kitchen truck when she emerged from the theater.

"Detective," Penelope said, "have you found Abigail?"

He shook his head. "No, but there's something about that last photo. I wanted to show you, see if you recognize anything strange."

Penelope pulled out her phone and opened the screenshot photo, enlarging the picture with her fingers. "What are you asking about?"

"You see that behind her?" Doyle asked.

Penelope squinted and tried to see what he meant. "It's the corner of a window, I think. But it's just a hazy sky."

"That's what I thought too," Doyle said. "But look again."

"Oh," Penelope said. "It's not a window. It's a mirror. And there's something..."

"Something in the corner, like an elbow maybe," Doyle said, "right there, hardly visible, but I can make it out."

Penelope enlarged the photo as much as she could, to the point where the picture didn't look like anything to her anymore. She shrunk it down some and eyed the person's arm. Slender and white, almost emaciated. She noticed something else resting on the counter that looked familiar but couldn't place it. "Who are you thinking this is?" Penelope asked.

"Hard to say," Doyle said. "Looks like a woman's elbow, right?"

Penelope looked again and shrugged. "It could be a thin man. Someone who doesn't eat regularly." Her head tilted slightly toward the direction of the homeless shelter.

"So what now?" she asked.

"We find her somehow, before it's too late."

CHAPTER 52

Penelope watched Detective Doyle cross the street and meet two pairs of uniformed officers in front of the apartment building. They intended to conduct a search of the entire building for any sign of Abigail.

"I don't expect her to be inside," Doyle said. "But we have to rule it out."

"Why not?" Penelope asked.

"Because in my experience, kidnappers usually move to a location that isn't connected to the victim. Makes them harder to track down."

Penelope nodded. "I guess that makes sense. What do they want? The kidnappers?"

"Apart from the money? That's anyone's guess."

After they went upstairs, Penelope checked on her crew and went over the supper menu with them.

"Let's keep it lighter, eliminate the red meat, since it doesn't seem too popular with this crowd," Penelope said.

"What do you want to do with the leftovers from yesterday?" Francis said, pulling out a half-full hotel pan of beautifully cooked top rounds.

"Wrap that up for me, will you?" Penelope asked. "I'm going to take it down to the shelter."

"You got it, Boss."

CHAPTER 53

While Penelope waited for Francis to package up some leftovers, she looked up at the building across the street, watching shadows flit across the glass, but unable to see anyone inside the open windows. Looking back at the sidewalk, she was surprised to see Mrs. Connor standing at the door, ringing the buzzer to be let inside.

"I'll be right back," Penelope said, dodging in between a couple of cars to cross the street. "Mrs. Connor?"

The woman looked around with a startled expression and gripped her handbag closer to her waist.

"Sorry, I didn't mean to scare you," Penelope said.

Mrs. Connor let out the breath she was holding. "I'm sorry, I'm just on edge lately."

"That's understandable," Penelope said. "How are you holding up?"

"I'm...I don't know. I just want to visit the room one more time," Mrs. Connor said meekly. "It's silly but I thought if I could see some of the girl's things, I could figure out who she might have been, what her connection to Elspeth is."

"They took most of her things away," Penelope said. "I did find some coasters she'd collected from bars and restaurants."

Mrs. Connor deflated a bit and sagged against the building wall. "Those wouldn't have been our Elspeth's. She didn't go to bars. Why is this happening to us?"

"I'm not sure. Hey, do you want to get a cup of coffee?" Penelope asked, reaching out to touch the woman's arm.

Mrs. Connor flinched at her touch, then gave her an embarrassed glance. "Sorry. Coffee would be nice. If it's not too much of a bother."

"Let's go down to the place on the corner, sit down for a minute," Penelope said.

Mrs. Connor gave her a cautious once over then nodded. They turned and headed to Common Grounds on the corner. Once inside Penelope pointed to a table near the window and went to the counter, ordering two black coffees.

Mrs. Connor smiled gratefully when Penelope set the cup down in front of her.

"You're very kind," Mrs. Connor said.

"It's the least I can do," Penelope said. "I can't imagine what you must be going through."

"It's a nightmare," she whispered before taking a sip from her cup. She winced at the heat then took another sip. "My husband is beside himself. Where could Elspeth be?"

"I wish they could tell you more," Penelope said sympathetically. "What was she like, you know, as a young girl?"

Mrs. Connor smiled and cupped her hands around the cup. Soft jazz music flowed around them in the room, and every few minutes a cold burst of air would circle their legs.

"She was a ball of energy growing up," Mrs. Connor said. "Always getting into things, very determined. Ever since my husband brought her home."

"Brought her home?" Penelope asked. "What do you mean?"

"She came to us in answer to our prayers," Mrs. Connor said sharply. "She was just tiny little thing. We raised her from an infant. He came through the door one night with that little bundle of joy in his arms. I fell in love with her immediately."

Penelope paused for a moment, then took a sip of coffee. "I'm sorry, if you don't mind my asking, who is Elspeth's birth mother?"

Mrs. Connor's cheeks reddened, then mellowed back to their pale hue. "My husband's first wife. She died in childbirth."

"I see," Penelope said.

Mrs. Connor spoke quickly. "My husband and I were not involved romantically until his wife passed away. We were good neighbors, that's all."

"Were you married too?" Penelope said.

"No."

"And you and Mr. Connor..."

"Were married soon after Elspeth came," Mrs. Connor said with a small smile.

"Did you ever meet Elspeth's mother before she died?"

"Yes, as I said, we were neighbors," Mrs. Connor said. "I knew her, and her family, Elspeth's aunt lives near us, her mother's sister. She's worried sick, too. Swears she had no idea of anything odd happening with our girl."

"Did Elspeth always want to dance?" Penelope asked.

"Oh, yes," Mrs. Connor said. "Even though her father discouraged it, didn't want any of this for her." She looked around at the coffee shop as if she was in a foreign country.

"Really?" Penelope asked. "What did he want her to be?"

"A wife," Mrs. Connor said with a smile. "I didn't see the harm in it, her twirling classes, then the ballet, and tap. I'm the one who took her to all of the lessons."

"Why didn't Mr. Connor want Elspeth to dance?" Penelope asked gently. "She's clearly really good at it."

"Elspeth's mother was a singer, her grandmother a dancer, for this show, as a matter of fact. They both always wanted to be famous," Mrs. Connor said. "It ended badly for both of them. My husband's first wife was always out at shows, singing. Not in church the way he wanted her to. His grandmother died alone in this god-awful city. He didn't want the same life for his daughter."

Penelope sat back in her chair and thought about what Mrs. Connor was saying. "That must have caused tension at home, if he was discouraging her from her dreams."

"Yes, and he has been angry with me ever since she got accepted to dance school," Mrs. Connor said.

"How does your husband get angry? Has he ever hit you or

Elspeth?"

Mrs. Connor's face hardened and she blushed. "That's none of your concern."

"Sorry," Penelope said, averting her eyes.

"I saw her in those sweet little tutus, all done up in pink, hair in pigtails. She'd laugh and twirl just like a little doll. She was such a happy child, I convinced him to let her do it. Now he'll never ever forgive me." She pulled her damp handkerchief from her pocket and swiped at her nose.

"I'm so sorry," Penelope said.

"To me she's still just a girl," Mrs. Connor said. "But I realize she's grown now and can make her own choices. And now she's gone. My husband didn't even want her to get that part time job after school. Said he wouldn't help her move here, either. But she'd saved enough on her own. And I slipped her some, that I'd hidden away."

"The police are working hard to find out what's happened to her." Penelope reached across the table.

Mrs. Connor reluctantly met her halfway, and grasped her fingers loosely with her own. "Either way, our lives will never be the same. My girl is gone."

CHAPTER 54

Penelope parted ways with Mrs. Connor and headed back toward the kitchen truck. She could hear faint music coming from inside the theater and recognized the number from being toward the middle of the show. She knew the performers would be taking a break after the matinee and would be ready to eat and rest before their second show later that night.

"Got that stuff wrapped up for you," Francis said when she stepped up inside. "And some young lady stopped by to see about some paperwork. Said she'd be back in twenty minutes."

Penelope rolled her eyes slightly. "Right. Chamay, the assistant."

"The who?" Francis asked with a smile.

"Never mind," Penelope said. She went back outside and pulled open the trucks' cab door, then rifled through a cardboard file keeper she stored behind the driver seat. She kept her blank forms in there, from permits to health inspection files and employment applications.

"When Chamay comes back, have her fill this out, please," Penelope said.

"We getting a new chef?" Francis asked.

"No," Penelope said. "It's for something else. I'm just helping Arlena out, getting Chamay's paperwork ready so she can get paid."

Penelope exchanged the paperwork for the package of leftover steak and headed toward the homeless shelter.

CHAPTER 55

Brandi greeted Penelope with a smile of recognition when she stepped into the lobby of the shelter.

"Got something for you, if you can use it," Penelope said. "Some nice quality steak we ordered too much of."

"Oh wow," Brandi said slowly as she stood up. "That's so nice of you."

A few of the men sitting in the common area craned their heads toward the front desk.

"Good," Penelope said. "I'm glad it won't go to waste. Hey, I have a question."

"Shoot."

"Do you know a woman named Helen Chadwick? She was the lady with Mother when I saw them out in New Jersey."

Brandi shrugged. "I know her to say hello. I haven't seen her around in a while, though."

Penelope deflated a bit at that.

"You know, I was thinking about you yesterday."

"Oh really?" Penelope asked.

"Something someone said," Brandi said. "I wrote it down." She rifled through a few things on her desk, and Penelope noticed her bookmark was already a quarter of the way through her new library book. "Folks was in here talking about all that's going on, with the theater and everything."

"Really?" Penelope asked.

"Yeah, you know, gossip and whatnot," Brandi said with a wave of her hand. "But then one of the overnighters said that the theater was no place for a woman to find a living, and that those girls got what was coming to them."

"What?" Penelope asked. "Who said that?"

Brandi narrowed her eyes and leaned in. "I don't know who said it, because I was into my book here and they were doing their chit chat over there with the TV turned up. I asked them who said that and didn't they have any sense, but no one owned up to it."

"Are you sure that's what you heard?" Penelope said.

"I'm pretty sure," Brandi said. "I was going to drop you a message, but then I thought, someone having an opinion isn't against the law, right?"

Penelope blew out a sigh and nodded. "Right."

The door opened and three homeless men, two wearing parkas and one wrapped in a dingy blanket stepped into the lobby.

"You all need to check in," Brandi said. "You know the drill."

"I'll let you go," Penelope said. "Call me if you think of anything else."

"Sure will," Brandi said. "And thanks for the steak. It will be much appreciated by everyone, I'm sure."

Penelope stepped around the men, who lumbered up to the desk to sign into the shelter. As she pushed her way out of the door, she smelled something odd, mixed in with the smell of unwashed bodies she'd passed in the foyer. The faint scent of roses drifted toward her and she turned on her heel to face the group of men.

"I forgot to ask you something," Penelope said, watching them. She approached the desk again as Brandi looked at her questioningly. "How do you like those books? I've been meaning to read them."

Brandi looked at her questioningly, then her expression relaxed with understanding. "They're good, you know. Nothing like a good PI story to keep the action moving."

"But do you have to begin at the first book?" Penelope asked, stepping closer to the group of men, who were mumbling to each other as they filled their names into the ledger. "Or can you start reading from anywhere?" She let her eyes drift to the men.

The last one stepped up to sign the book, and Penelope noticed the one closest to her was frozen still, his dark hoodie pulled around his small torso and obscuring his face. A long wiry beard poured out onto his chest, and his elbows were rigid under his sweatshirt.

"You can read any of them, I guess," Brandi said, following Penelope's gaze to the man standing quietly still. Penelope recognized him as the one who had approached Francis the other day, the one who made her feel uneasy looking down from the apartment windows.

Penelope took another step closer. Suddenly the smallest man bolted from his spot, and lunged toward her. Taken off guard, Penelope spun out of the way as he pushed past her toward the front door.

"Hey!" one of his companions shouted. "You're gonna miss dinner!"

Penelope felt a searing pain on her forearm and looked down, seeing a line of blood through a cut in her jacket. "He cut me," she said, watching the blood darken her sleeve.

The man banged through the door and was gone, the soft smell of roses drifting on the air behind him.

CHAPTER 56

"I don't know who that dude was. Just hooked up with us at the park this morning, then made our way down to the shelter for a meal. We ain't friends. He didn't talk hardly at all," the taller man who had been with Penelope's assailant explained to Detective Doyle.

Penelope held her arm with her opposite hand, a thick white bandage wrapped around her forearm.

"We should get you to the hospital," the EMT said to Penelope as he finished wrapping her arm. "You're going to need stitches."

"Great," Penelope said. "I've cut myself worse in the kitchen. Are you sure?"

"Well," he said, "at least a couple, I think."

Penelope sighed. "I should have run after him."

"And get slashed worse?" Detective Doyle said. "Do me a favor and stop helping so much. You're in danger, I told you."

"I was surrounded by people," Penelope protested. "I always am."

"It only takes a second," Doyle said. "As you can see."

"Brandi," Penelope said. "Has he been here before?"

Brandi shook her head but hesitated. "I mean, I don't think so, but I'm not here twenty-four seven. The night shift guy will be here in a few hours. You should ask him too."

"What name did he sign in with?" Doyle asked, looking at the ledger.

"Chaz," Doyle said, looking at the register. "And a scribble. Maybe Na is the last name? Or it begins with N A and he stopped writing for some reason."

"You know anyone named Chaz?" Doyle asked Penelope.

"I don't think so," Penelope said.

"Okay, get her to the ER, and then you should go home and stay safe," Doyle said.

Penelope nodded and stayed silent, then allowed the EMT to lead her out the front door.

CHAPTER 57

Penelope was back in her kitchen truck two hours later. The doctor at the hospital confirmed she'd suffered a deep scratch that caused significant bleeding on her forearm, but she could get away with some suture glue and butterfly bandages at the deepest part. Her jacket had protected her from a deeper cut, for which she was grateful.

"Penny," a familiar voice called from outside the truck.

Penelope's heart skipped a beat and she looked down at her bandaged arm. "Joey?" She ducked her head through the service window and saw him there, a look of concern on his face.

She thought about looking for her spare jacket in the front of her truck to cover her arm, but decided if he had tracked her down in Manhattan and had that expression on his face, he probably already knew what had happened. Bad news travels fast, especially in the brotherhood of police officers.

"Hey," Penelope said happily. "I'll be right out."

Joey stood with his hands on his hips, swiveling at the waist and taking in the alley where her truck was parked.

"Hey man," Francis waved from the window.

"You're supposed to be taking care of her when I'm not around," Joey said.

Francis grimaced and shrugged his shoulders then turned back to the grill.

"It's nothing," Penelope said, holding out her arm. "I'll be healed up in no time."

Joey grabbed her and hugged her close, careful not to hold her arm between them.

"Is there somewhere we can talk?" Joey asked.

"Um," Penelope wavered. She held the belief it was never going to be a good topic when people asked if they could talk. "Sure, let's go upstairs to the suite. I think most of the crew is inside the theater getting set up for tonight's show."

They went across the street and rode up the elevator in near silence, Joey rubbing Penelope's shoulders and her leaning into his strong shoulder.

Penelope let them into the suite, and they headed to the bedroom when they saw one of the editors working on a monitor in the main room. She raised a hand in a distracted wave, not hearing them through her headphones.

Joey and Penelope sat on the edge of the bed, Penelope looking at her hands clasped in her lap and Joey gazing out the window.

"What did you want to talk about?" Penelope said.

Joey hesitated a few second then began. "I want you to come home. Francis can handle this, and your other guys. Hire another chef, if you need to, but I would feel better if were safe back in New Jersey."

Something gave in her chest and she looped her uninjured arm around his broad shoulders.

"I don't want you to worry about me," Penelope said.

"Then come home," Joey insisted. "Let me protect you."

Penelope placed her head on his shoulder and he pulled her closer to him on the bed. He tilted her chin up and kissed her on the lips, then pulled away to look at her face.

"I can't just leave, Joey," Penelope said. "I said I'd do this project for Arlena and Randall and Max. Plus, there's a missing girl, and for some reason the person who has her is texting me about it." She pulled out and showed Joey the saved photo of Abigail.

"Doyle has this in hand, my friend assured me, he's a good man. And the Madisons will understand if you want to quit," Joey said. "You've been attacked."

"It was my fault," Penelope said, holding up her arm. "I pushed him when I could have just walked out and waited to see who he was. It was stupid of me to engage him like that."

"You're not stupid and it's not your fault some low life took a blade to you," Joey said, his voice rising an octave.

"But you understand I don't want to walk away from a promise?" Penelope said.

Joey sighed and gently untangled from her, then walked to the window. After a few minutes of staring down at the theater he said, "What have I gotten myself into with you, Penny Blue? You're the most important person in my life, and all I want to do is keep you safe."

Penelope stood up and went to his side, then leaned into him again. "I promise to be more careful. I don't want to get hurt either."

Joey shifted his eyes toward her and said, "I know I can't make you do anything, which is part of the reason I fell in love with you. But I can do my best to protect you."

"You do a great job at that," Penelope said.

"I had a feeling you'd respond the way you did, so I took the next couple of days off. I'm going to be your new apprentice on the truck. You can teach me all your fancy knife skills, boss me around. And in the meantime, I will watch your back."

Penelope laughed. "Are you sure you want to join the Red Carpet Catering team? I'm a pretty tough boss."

Joey looked down at her arm. "I know how tough you can be. I'm ready for you." He turned and looped his arms around her waist and kissed her again. Soon they were back on the bed, tugging at each other's shirts. Penelope was vaguely aware of the outer door of the suite opening again and pulled away from Joey, straightening her clothes and running her fingers through her hair.

"I'm at work," Penelope said.

Joey cleared his throat. "You're right. Boss."

Penelope slapped him lightly on the shoulder as someone knocked on the bedroom door.

"Come in," Penelope said.

Chamay opened the door and walked in, holding a few papers in her hand. "Miss Sutherland, I have that paperwork Arlena asked for. That man on the truck downstairs said you were up here."

Penelope stood up from the bed. "You found me."

Chamay handed over the paperwork and Penelope glanced at the first line. "Wait, this isn't your name."

"Oh," Chamay laughed. "Yeah, it's my legal name, the one I'd need the checks to be written to."

"So, Charlene Mason is your real name, then," Penelope said.

"Yes, I changed it," Chamay said. "There's already a Charlene Mason with a Screen Actors Guild card, and there can't be two of us."

"But you're not an actress," Penelope said.

"Not yet," Chamay said with a roll of her eyes. "I'm one step closer now." She eyed the paperwork and then Penelope.

"You know that as Arlena's assistant you'll be running for coffee, and walking her dog, answering the phone at all hours and booking travel arrangements? It's not an acting job."

"Oh, I know," Chamay said. "But it's not what you know, it's who you know, right?"

"I suppose," Penelope said.

"Ta to you as well, sir," Chamay said as she turned and bounced out the door.

Joey waved his hand in a half wave as she closed the door. "And who was that chipper young woman?"

"I'm not sure," Penelope said, staring at the documents in her hand. "An assistant with a stage name."

"Do you know what Cary Grant's real name was?" Joey asked.

"It's not Cary Grant?"

"No, it's Archibald Leach," Joey said with slight exasperation.

"What? I've never heard that," Penelope said. "You and your classic movie channel trivia."

"I like the classics," Joey said. "A lot of people use a different name in the business."

Penelope's eyes fell on the file boxes lined up against the wall and something clicked. "I wonder how many use not just a different name, but a different identity."

"What?" Joey asked, following her gaze. "What's in there?"

"The history of the Vitrine," Penelope said.

"But the crimes are happening now," Joey said. "How is information from..." he eyed one of the boxes "...1946 going to help you solve the killing and disappearance of Big Apple Dancers of today?"

"The past has a way of creeping up on us," Penelope said. "Plus, Elspeth isn't really Elspeth." She tapped her finger on her chin. "Where do you think the real Elspeth went?"

"Well, you said the deceased girl was using her identity, and didn't you say she seemed flush with cash?" Joey asked.

"Yeah, and she was a bit of a scam artist maybe," Penelope said. "What if...what if Elspeth got herself to the city, then just wanted to disappear."

"Or she was made to disappear by someone taking over her identity," Joey said.

"But that doesn't explain the money fully," Penelope said. "I get the impression from getting to know her family it wasn't always great at home."

"But she made it here," Joey said. "Why would she want to disappear after she'd gotten to her goal?"

"Maybe to get away from her family permanently?" Penelope thought about the times she'd seen Mr. Connor's anger in the past few days, and about what Mrs. Connor had said in the coffee shop, about how Elspeth's father wanted a different life for her.

"Seems an overly elaborate scheme," Joey said. "Why not just run away?"

"If you run away, people come looking for you," Penelope said. "Maybe she swapped identities with a girl, Cassie Chadwick, and then just slipped away, getting a head start? But something happened, Cassie didn't hold up her end of the bargain...but if she had it might have been a year before anyone knew Elspeth was gone."

"Her parents wouldn't have come and seen her perform?"

Penelope shook her head. "Her father especially did not support this career, or her lifestyle choices. He wanted her to stay close to home, live a more traditional life."

"But it Elspeth wanted this so badly, would she just give up her dream of dancing in New York?" Joey asked.

"Maybe it was worth it to be out on her own, or she decided to go about it in a different way," Penelope said. "She's just starting out, she didn't have a career to lose yet."

Penelope set Chamay's paperwork on the bed and went to one of the boxes in the middle of the pile and pulled it out. "Let's look at the 1970s."

"What are we looking for?" Joey asked.

"Any connection to Elspeth," Penelope said. "Maybe we'll find another sort of ghost haunting the Vitrine Theater."

CHAPTER 58

The next morning Joey drove them into the city in his police cruiser. "I can park on the street and no one will bother it," he said. They were able to miss the biggest push of rush hour over the bridge because there was no matinee that day, so they only had to arrive early afternoon.

Penelope's arm ached a bit, but she was grateful it wasn't a worse injury and wouldn't affect her work too much. Plus, she had an extra set of strong hands on the set that day. When she thought about Joey in her kitchen truck in an apron wielding a spatula, she smiled every time.

"Uh oh," she said, reading the news on her phone. She'd scanned the news sections of all the local papers for any news on Abigail. She hadn't seen any more vanishing texts from the anonymous sender either.

"What's up?" Joey asked, keeping his eyes on the road.

"Nothing," Penelope said. "Well, on *Page Six* they're talking about the Madisons again, about how they're not getting along on the set of their behind-the-scenes documentary at the theater."

"What? Are they not getting along?" Joey asked.

"I think they're fine," Penelope said. "It's a bit frantic, and they're working out their roles, but they've just started."

"The papers have to print something," Joey said with an irritated wave of his hand. Sometimes Penelope could picture him as a much older man, and the thought warmed her heart and made her chuckle at the same time.

"Were you able to find anything out about Elspeth's finances?"

Penelope asked. She'd seen him working on his laptop at the kitchen island the night before and hoped he was able to uncover something.

"Clarissa is looking into the financials, whatever accounts in her name we can find. And she's pulling a credit check on any new accounts opened, addresses, things like that."

"She's not going to mind?" Penelope asked. "She's always so by the book."

"Nah, she likes me now," Joey said. "We do favors for each other. Plus, it's for a case. She's a crime fighter first and foremost."

Their search through the first few years of the seventies didn't yield any familiar names or faces. The photographs were all turning sepia, so everyone had an orange glow that started to look normal after the third box.

"It was the kind of photo processing they used back in the day," Joey explained. "My parents have old albums with pictures like that, uncles and stuff."

"I'm glad they figured out how to fix that," Penelope said. "Although it was kind of cool to see the world in Technicolor, or whatever you call it."

"Lots of big hair," Joey said. "And flimsy costumes. Like that iconic Farrah Fawcett poster."

"Another sign of the times, before they discovered thicker lining for bathing suits," Penelope said. "I can't believe the Snow Queen wore that same Christmas tree head thing all the way back then."

"Tradition," Joey said with a shrug. He pulled into a spot outside the apartment building and tucked his police parking card on the dash before locking the car and heading with Penelope over to the alley.

The truck was locked up tight, and the iron gate secure. Penelope pulled out her keys and opened the gate, ushering her newest chef inside and then locking it up behind them.

"Let's see you make an omelette," Penelope said once they were inside.

"Seriously?" Joey asked.

"Yes," Penelope said, pointing at the grill.

A half hour later Penelope and Joey shared a spinach, mushroom and goat cheese omelette and she felt certain he could help out sufficiently on the truck and not get in the way during the rush.

"Delicious," Penelope said, then kissed him on the cheek.

"No flirting when I'm on the clock," Joey warned. He wiped his hands on his apron and shook Francis's hand as he entered the kitchen.

"Warning, Boss," Francis said in a low voice. "Miss Madison is fired up about something and she's on the way over."

Penelope sighed, and tried to think what it might be.

"Did you see that crap in the paper?" Arlena asked. Penelope had come out of the truck and met her in front of the coffee urn on the table behind it.

"Oh, the thing about you and your dad not getting along?" Penelope asked. "Yeah, I saw it."

"Who gave them that information?" Arlena asked.

Penelope thought for a second. "I don't know. But maybe the question is why would someone give them that tip?"

Arlena looked at her and raised her palms in the air. "I have no idea. Max and Daddy want this project to be successful, it's for our family. I trust you implicitly."

"Well, any publicity is good publicity?"

"Maybe. But I'd rather focus on how we've hired a crew that employs all women. Something positive."

"If it's not you, and it's not me, who else might—" Penelope said.

"Sybil!" Arlena hissed. "She was there both times when news was leaked about the family."

"But why would she do that?"

"To sabotage me!" Arlena said. "It's not enough to marry into the family, now she wants to take it over."

"Oh, I don't think Sybil would do that," Penelope said.

"Hmm," Arlena said. "We'll see."

"What are you going to do?" Penelope asked.

"I'm going to bury the lead," Arlena said. "Give her some false information on purpose and see if it shows up anywhere." She pulled out her phone and began texting. "I'm going to get her down here and set the trap."

"Okay," Penelope said. "We've got a show to do here too, right? Maybe we should focus on that."

"Pen," Arlena said patiently. "I know you think I'm acting like a spoiled child..."

"I'm not saying..."

Arlena held up her hand. "I know what I sound like. It's just that we can't have someone in the family who is going to ruin our reputations on purpose."

Penelope's phone buzzed in her pocket and she pulled it out. "Oh no. I got another one. Joey!" She began taking screenshots of her phone again before the picture could dissolve away. Abigail appeared to be asleep, her face bruised, her cheek black and blue.

Joey stepped down from the truck and looked at her phone. "Can you forward it?"

"I don't think so," Penelope said. "It disappears before you can do anything. There's no instructions on how to pay either."

"Is she okay?" Arlena asked, looking over their shoulders.

"It doesn't look like it," Joey said. "Someone needs to find this girl. Whoever has her doesn't sound like they know what they're doing. Or they're unbalanced."

Penelope stared at the picture as it melted from the screen, her eyes dancing around the photo. "There," she said, pointing to a round disk on the dresser next to the bed. "I recognize that logo. I know where that's from."

After the photo faded away a message appeared: *Pay or #3 Dies.*

The three of them stared at the words for a second, then Penelope dialed the number for Detective Doyle.

"I'm heading to the Tavern now," Doyle said. "You stay put."

CHAPTER 59

"We can't close down the Vitrine Theater based on a threat from some unknown person," Armand said from behind his desk.

"You yourself have been attacked right here," Penelope said. "You know this isn't an idle threat. This person is killing people."

"But why?" Armand said. "Who would have a problem with a Christmas show, a fun event for the whole family?"

Penelope put her hands on his desk and leaned forward. She'd come up after calling Doyle, who said he was on his way over after stopping by the Tavern.

"Think about it," Penelope said. "Someone has a big problem with this place. What are they upset about?"

"I have no idea, I assure you," Armand said. He sat back in his chair and crossed his arms. His words were confident, but his expression agitated and doubtful. "I can't respond to these threats. What would you have me do? Shutter the doors and put all of these people out of work? The carpenters, the musicians, all of the girls?"

"To save a life, maybe go dark for a night or two until the police can find Abigail. Before she turns up dead like the others. Isn't her life worth something to you?"

Armand stood up from his chair and straightened his jacket. "You put me in an impossible situation. I'm sorry, the answer is no. The show will go on as planned."

CHAPTER 60

Penelope walked slowly down the stairs and through the dressing rooms, glancing at the girls as they passed her in the narrow hallway. The energy was always high among the dancers, like they lived on a different plane, one that was in constant motion.

On her way to the break room, she overheard snippets of conversations behind the curtains, and the odd note of music from someone's phone as they got into costume for the matinee show.

"...took me out to dinner, but then he thought that meant..."

"...trying this new protein powder. I think it's working..."

"...last time she was in Phoenix it snowed..."

Penelope stopped short outside one of the dressing rooms. "Excuse me?" she said, peeking in behind the curtain. Meredith, the current Snow Queen, was chatting on her phone. She held up a hand, her long red fingernails catching the lights from her makeup mirror. The soft glittery powder on her skin against her dark hair made her look like a real snow queen.

"Hang on a second, Mom," Meredith said, placing the phone against her chest. "Can I help you, Penelope?" She smiled sweetly. "Oh, I have to tell you, I love the marinade you used for the chicken yesterday. So yummy."

"Thanks," Penelope said. "Sorry to interrupt."

Meredith looked at her expectantly.

"Did you say something about snow in Phoenix?"

Meredith looked confused for a second, then seemed to remember. "Yes, I was telling my mom about all of the things...you know that are happening here." Her brow crinkled with worry for a second, then smoothed back out. "And I was saying the last time I spoke with Elspeth, who wasn't really Elspeth, I guess, she was talking about how snowy it gets in Phoenix.

"Well, my mom here," she nodded at the phone she held against her chest, "says it snows there all the time. Because it's in upstate New York. She's originally from Rochester, and Phoenix is a small town nearby, right on Lake Ontario."

Something clicked in Penelope's brain. "Thank you, Meredith. And thank your mom!"

CHAPTER 61

Penelope stepped onto the kitchen truck and yanked the door closed behind her. The wind was biting that day, and the sky was dark. The smell of snow was in the air.

"Phoenix, New York," Penelope said to Joey. He was slicing tomatoes on the cutting board, much slower than a trained chef typically would, but his knife work was uniform and precise.

"Where?" Joey asked.

"Upstate New York," Penelope said. "I'm going back upstairs to look at those boxes again. I remember seeing one of the Snow Queens from back then was Miss New York, from somewhere upstate. Cassie Chadwick went to school in Phoenix." She pulled out her phone and googled the town. "Maybe that's the connection to the theater."

"Maybe," Joey said. He pulled another tomato from the bin and went to work on slicing it. "Hey, Clarissa got back to me on the money thing. Elspeth hasn't opened a new account in the last year, she only has her bank account her parents opened for her when she was underage."

"That's weird, right?" Penelope said. "She's a grown woman on her own and she still has an account overseen by her parents?"

"Looks that way," Joey said.

"But, how do you rent a car, or put a deposit down for anything without a credit card in your own name?" Penelope asked.

"It's a possibility that if this girl wanted to disappear she could've purchased a new identity somehow. It's not as hard to do as you might think."

"She doesn't have much of a virtual footprint," Penelope said. "No social media to speak of, nothing to trace her by."

"If something was happening back in Seattle, and she wanted to get away for good, it's possible she did just that."

"And swapped identities with Cassie Chadwick, aka Elspeth?" Penelope asked.

"Yeah," Joey said. "No one comes looking as long as things are going well, and after enough time, you can be gone. Really gone."

Penelope went into the suite, past the crew working in the main room and into the bedroom.

"Oh, hi guys," Penelope said. Jackson and Dakota were propped on the bed playing with their iPads. "Where's your mom?"

"Powdering her nose," Dakota said with a smile, then went back to focusing on her screen.

Penelope pulled out the box labeled 1975 and opened it.

"Hmm," Penelope said. "That's weird."

"What?" Jackson said distractedly. He tapped on his device with his finger.

"It's almost empty," Penelope said. "All of the other boxes have lots of photos. This one..." She reached in and pulled out a photo book and opened it. A yellowed newspaper article fell out, the headline reading *Snow Queen Severely Injured in Fall.*

A group shot of all of the dancers from that year was on the first page, and Penelope scanned through the names. Seeing no familiar ones, she looked at the faces one by one.

The Snow Queen smiled back at her from the photo taken over forty years earlier. She was just as pretty as all of the other years. Her hair was a soft wave of gold over her forehead with the Christmas tree head ornament perched on top. The name printed beneath the photo caused Penelope to suck in a breath: C. Connor.

"She looks just like Elspeth," Penelope muttered. "This must be her grandmother," Penelope said.

"Penelope," Sybil said from the doorway, causing her to jump.

"We're not in your way here, are we?"

Penelope closed the photo album and shook her head. "No, of course not."

"What are you doing?" Sybil said, looking at the book in her hands.

"Just some research. We'll have lunch ready to go in a little bit. You should bring the kids down."

"That's a good idea," Sybil said. "We came in today to get some shopping done, right guys?"

"Yes, Mother," Jackson sighed.

"I wanted to ask you something," Sybil said, pulling Penelope aside for a moment.

"What's up?" Penelope asked.

"Do you think I should convince Randall to postpone our wedding until next year?"

"Oh, I'm not...why are you asking me?" Penelope stammered.

"Well, you know, you and Arlena are close. I was thinking you'd know if she'd be, how do I put it...happier if we weren't in competition for her big day."

Penelope thought for a moment before responding. "I think Arlena is happy for you both, and you should do what you want. It's nice of you to consider her feelings, but you deserve to be happy too."

Sybil put a hand on Penelope's shoulder. "Thank you, Penelope. You've always got such sensible advice."

Penelope heard a swooshing sound from Jackson's iPad.

"I've got to run now," Penelope said. "See you downstairs."

CHAPTER 62

Penelope walked through Central Park, the first flakes of snow falling from the sky and landing softly on her knit hat and the shoulders of her coat. They were predicting a half a foot of snow, and she wondered how that might affect that evening's theater goers. New Yorkers were a tough crowd and didn't let a little snow derail their plans, but she knew the show attracted many tourists who might not want to make the trek.

Penelope entered the Tavern and headed straight for the main bar, barely acknowledging the hostess as she passed through the door. As she rounded the corner, she saw the bartender on duty was a tall blonde woman with a deeply tanned face, despite the season.

"What can I get for you, ma'am?" she asked cordially.

"Cup of coffee, please," Penelope said.

"Coming right up."

"Is the other bartender, Derek, here?"

"No, he called out and I'm covering for him."

"Oh," Penelope said, picking up a nearby cardboard coaster. "Does he do that a lot? Call off work, I mean?"

She shrugged. "He had the flu last winter and I picked up a few of his shifts. Once he begged me to cover so he could make an audition for a TV show. He didn't get the part. Otherwise he's pretty reliable."

"So Derek's an actor?"

The bartender scoffed. "He's a bartender who takes acting classes."

"Did a detective stop by earlier?" Penelope asked as casually as possible.

"Not at the bar. Maybe one of the managers would know."

Penelope eyed the coaster, and pictured Abigail, tied up in the chair with the very same one next to her on the table.

"Why are you asking about Derek?" She placed a cup of coffee on the bar in front of Penelope and carefully placed a stirring spoon on the saucer. Even her hands were tan, her fingernails gelled hot pink.

"I'm checking a reference," Penelope lied.

"Really?" She brushed a strand of her blonde bang from her eyelashes. "Derek's looking to move jobs?"

"No, it's for an acquaintance of his," Penelope said evasively.

"Who, his girlfriend?" she asked.

"Yes. Have you met her?"

"I think she's an ex now," she admitted. "She came in one day, yelling at him back here. The manager told him if she came back in he would have to find another place to work."

"What were they arguing about?"

"Same old," the bartender said knowingly. "She caught him with another woman. A friend of hers, from what I could make out. He got caught red handed, in bed with her."

"Really?" Penelope asked. Her heart was beating faster but she kept her expression calm.

"Yeah, I didn't see the argument. But word gets around this place pretty quick. Derek's good looking but he's a bit on the creepy side, if you ask me. I caught him taking pictures of young girls in the park out back once. Like, who does that except a straight up creeper?" She glanced down at her blouse. "He's always accidently brushing up again the women here. You know, the usual. Customers too. When I heard he had a girlfriend, I thought, well, maybe he's not all the way bad, and then she comes in and confirms I was right all along."

"Derek lives in the city, right?" Penelope asked.

"In a dive in Hell's Kitchen, with a bunch of other guys," she said, rolling her eyes. "He invited me to a party there one time. I said I was busy."

"You know the address?" Penelope asked.

The bartender eyed her for a minute. "You really know his girlfriend or are you some kind of bill collector?"

Penelope laughed and relaxed her shoulders. She picked up her spoon and swirled it through her coffee. "Actually, I'm a chef, and he asked me for a background check reference. I'm just making sure I'm not sticking my neck out too far. It's a favor to his girlfriend, an old employee of mine."

"So Abigail used to cook for you."

Penelope dropped her spoon onto the saucer with a clatter. "Who?"

"Abigail, his girlfriend. Well, ex-girlfriend now, since she caught him cheating with her friend."

CHAPTER 63

"He's in Hell's Kitchen, and I think he has Abigail," Penelope said into the phone as she rushed back down Broadway from the park.

"How do you know?" Detective Doyle said. The street noise drowned out some of what he said.

"Abigail was his girlfriend. Remember she said she'd broken up with her boyfriend when she got to the city? I assumed she meant back at home. I didn't think they were both already here." She rattled off the address she'd gotten from the bartender at the tavern.

"Okay, it's worth a look. I'll send a squad car."

"One other thing," Penelope said. "His coworker said Abigail broke up with him because she caught him cheating with her friend."

"Okay..." Doyle said.

"What if it was with Elspeth?"

Penelope thought back to her first visit to the Tavern, tried to picture Derek's reaction to the news of Elspeth's death. He seemed surprised, at least to her. But he was an acting student, too.

Penelope's heart pumped along with her legs as she turned every few feet to look for a taxi. The snow was coming down harder and the avenue was jammed with cars, busses and cabs, all of which had their lights off.

She decided just to walk the final ten blocks. Her hair was damp from the snow, but she was warm all over from the exertion and the knowledge that she might have finally found Abigail.

*   *   *

When she arrived at the Vitrine, the line of theater patrons was as robust as always. Many of the theater goers held up umbrellas against the snow. Rounding the corner, she saw Joey shoveling a path from the kitchen truck to the back door of the theater.

"There she is," Joey said, pausing his shoveling to take in Penelope. "You're soaked."

She hugged him tight, their coats putting a thick boundary between them. "I think I might have found Abigail."

"Wow," Joey said. "Where?"

"If I'm right, she's in an apartment in Hell's Kitchen. Doyle is sending a car over there now."

"I won't ask how you figured it out," Joey said. "And I'll assume you're still being careful."

The back door of the theater opened and Meredith stuck her head out.

"Excuse me," she said. "But you haven't seen my tiara, have you?"

"Your Christmas headdress?" Penelope said.

"Wardrobe has misplaced it, I guess," Meredith said. "I thought since you're all around the theater all the time you might have come across it."

"I haven't seen it, sorry," Penelope said.

Meredith, who was wearing her shimmery white dress, stepped outside. "I don't think I can go on without it. I don't want to be the first Snow Queen without a crown."

Penelope's phone pinged, and she pulled it from her coat pocket. "I'll tell the guys to keep an eye out for it."

"Thanks," Meredith said. She went back inside, the door slamming behind her.

"Did you get a new message?" Joey asked. "Another picture of Abigail?"

"No, it's a text from Doyle," Penelope said. "Abigail wasn't at the apartment. Or Derek either. But the murder weapon was—the serrated knife used in both killings."

"Who is Derek?" Joey asked.

"He's a bartender at the Tavern," Penelope said.

Another message came through as she was putting her phone away. It was just one word: *Pickles.*

CHAPTER 64

Penelope and Joey walked to the homeless shelter on the corner and glanced inside the door.

"I'm not sure what's going on," Penelope said. "But that's Brandi's code word."

Joey reached around to his waistband and felt his concealed weapon there. "Let's think it's nothing, but be ready for anything."

Penelope pulled open the door and Brandi gave her a small nod and stood up from her chair.

"Miss Penelope," Brandi said. "Did you bring us more steaks? We sure did enjoy that last batch. Who's your friend?" Her eyes slid to the common room and back to Penelope.

Penelope glanced over too and saw a familiar jacket. The person's back was to her as they looked up at the television screen. Someone else was sitting in a nearby chair, but otherwise the space was empty.

"This is my..." Penelope began, "sous chef. Joseph."

"Okay," Brandi said.

The man in the common room turned toward them, his wiry beard and hood obscuring his face.

"I was thinking, we needed to thank you for your generosity," Brandi said. She stared, talking faster.

Joey wandered over to the common area, pretending like he was interested in something on the television. A police siren sounded outside and the man in the hoodie turned around to face the door.

Penelope caught a flash of his eyes right before he bolted,

running hard into Joey and pushing him away. Penelope pressed herself against Brandi's desk.

"I told you it was him!" Brandi shouted as he banged through the front door.

Penelope and Joey followed him through the door. The man darted around slower moving people on the sidewalk, his tarp coat billowing out around him.

"He's heading for the theater," Penelope said, picking up her pace. Her breath was short, and even though she was a regular runner, the sprint was taking the wind out of her quickly. Joey huffed beside her.

The man ducked into the alley behind the theater and disappeared from their sight. When Penelope neared the entrance, she startled a woman who turned around quickly and accidentally struck Penelope in the face with her umbrella.

"Some street person just ran inside, Boss," Francis said, a covered hotel pan in his hands. "Right in through the back door."

"Stay out here," Penelope said. "That's the guy who stabbed me."

A police car pulled up behind them and Detective Doyle got out. "Hold up," he shouted, but Penelope was already through the door.

CHAPTER 65

The theater was filling with patrons, and the orchestra warming up. The dressing rooms were abuzz with activity and dancers rushed to and fro. Wardrobe was calling to the individual dancers to line up for costume inspections. Martha was shouting last minute words of encouragement to her girls.

"What is going on?" Armand demanded when he saw Penelope rush through the curtains and onto the stage. The outer one was still drawn across the stage, so they were hidden from the audience.

Penelope huffed and held up her injured arm. "The man who attacked me is in this theater somewhere."

"I haven't seen anyone," Armand said, looking around in alarm.

Penelope looked up and pointed at the scaffolding above their heads. "He's there."

"Oh my," Armand said. "We can't have that, not for a minute. We're about to draw the curtain."

Joey ran to the nearest ladder and began to climb. Penelope went to follow him.

"Wait," Detective Doyle shouted behind her. "You stay put."

Penelope thought about ignoring him, but then She got down from the ladder and stepped back.

"He's heading for the office," Penelope said, pointing. Joey was a few feet under him and catching up.

"I see him," Doyle said. He pulled his radio from his belt and spoke into it quickly.

Just then the man stopped and gazed down at them. He raised

his arms out to each side, as if he was about to take flight, then brought them down and tore off his jacket. It fell to the ground near Doyle's feet.

Pausing on one of the catwalks, he then stepped out of his boots and pulled off his socks.

"What's he doing?" Joey asked. "A strip tease?"

A couple of uniformed officers joined them on the stage, and most of the dancers stood off to the side, all of the chattering and activity coming to silence as they watched the homeless man remove his pants, then his shirt.

"He's wearing one of our costumes," one of the dancers said.

Penelope stared transfixed as he began tugging on his hair, flinging a long wig to the ground, and then shed his long scraggly beard.

"Abigail!" Penelope said. "Abigail, you're safe! Come down."

Abigail smiled sadly down at them, then twirled once around in a perfect pirouette, the pulled herself up on the railing, teetering on the narrow board.

A few gasps escaped the group of dancers. "She's going to fall," one of them murmured.

"Abigail," Martha said, stepping toward the center of the stage. "Please come down and let's talk about it."

"I can't talk to you," Abigail shouted. "You don't listen."

"Please, dear," Martha said. "It's going to be okay. Come down please."

Joey had paused at the catwalk beneath Abigail after she'd stepped up on the rail. Two of Doyle's officers had made their way to Armand's office, and were attempting to climb down to her from the balcony.

Abigail stepped back down to the catwalk and knelt down, throwing aside a piece of curtain. She turned back around, a glimmering tiara in her hands.

"It's my crown," Meredith said. "What's she doing with it?"

Abigail slipped the Christmas tree headdress on and adjusted it, her wavy blonde hair falling in waves over her shoulders. Her eye was still blackened, and her cheeks bruised, as if from a beating. Penelope hoped it was just stage makeup, maybe part of her disguise.

Doyle mumbled to another officer who hurried away.

"Okay, Abigail, we see you now," Doyle said. "It's time to come down from there. Come on, now."

Abigail smiled down at him. "What is the point of coming down? I've lost my spot, the one I've worked for my whole life."

"You didn't lose it," Martha said. She clasped her hands together and held them up toward Abigail, begging her. "You can stay here, my dear. Of course you can."

"You cut me from the show," Abigail said. "Because I wasn't getting better fast enough. And I took that job, for just one day."

"You did what?" Armand asked Martha.

"I wasn't available for rehearsal, so I was cut from the show," Abigail said. "I've lost everything. I never should have come here."

"Look, if you come down now, we can work something out," Martha said. Armand looked at her like she'd lost her mind.

"We want you to stay here with us," Martha pleaded.

"Lie," Abigail said. "There are ten girls behind me, waiting to fill the spot. Dancing, and everywhere else. Pay the ransom and I'll leave."

"My dear, you must come down, show or no show," Armand said. "Stop this nonsense now. It's not safe up there, and you know that."

"Yes, Mr. Wagner," Abigail said. "We all know how safe you like to keep your dancers."

Armand's face reddened. "Of course I do. What are you implying?"

"You dropped her on purpose," Abigail said.

"The girl is obviously gone mad," Armand said to Doyle. "She's talking nonsense."

"You dropped her. She died right here on this stage," Abigail said. She grabbed onto one of the railings and hoisted herself back onto the ledge of the scaffolding. "I know the whole story."

Joey looked down at Doyle, who motioned for him to stay put.

"You know nothing," Armand said. "It was an accident."

"Step back off the railing, Abigail," Doyle said. "It's too dangerous." He looked around the stage at all of the group of onlookers.

"Nobody cares if I get hurt," Abigail said. She took her hand from the railing and Penelope's stomach lurched. "One injury and I'm taken off the A line. Dream over."

"We've got Derek down at the station," Doyle said. "He told us what happened."

Abigail faltered. "It wasn't me. It's his fault! If he hadn't...she was my friend, my one friend here. If he hadn't dropped me for her...and you," she glared at Martha, "hadn't dropped me for her...none of this would've happened."

"Abigail, we can figure this out," Penelope urged. "I know you cared about Elspeth."

"You mean Cassie?" Abigail asked. "I'm not going to jail because of him. He killed them both, it wasn't me."

Abigail smiled sadly and spread her arms wide, swan diving off of the scaffolding toward stage. Joey reached out to grab for her, his fingers grazing her calf as she fell past him.

Screams erupted from the group of onlookers as Abigail bounced onto the curtain, pulled tight by the police officer and members of the orchestra.

CHAPTER 66

"How did you guess the bartender knew Abigail?" Joey asked. They were sitting on the bumper of the kitchen truck, their knees touching.

"I didn't," Penelope said. "I saw the coaster from the Tavern, the same one that Elspeth swiped from his bar. I went there to ask him if Abigail had ever been in there before, and who she might have been with. I was trying to find her."

A police car idled in the alley. Abigail was inside, her head hanging toward her lap, her shoulders shuddering.

"Why kill Cassie?" Joey asked.

Detective Doyle stepped out from the theater, the sound of loud Christmas music following him through the door. It slammed shut behind him. "Jealousy," he said. "Derek slept with Cassie up there," he tossed a glance at the apartment building across the street. "Abigail was supposed to be gone at an audition but felt sick and came home. An argument happened, and Cassie was knocked unconscious. Cassie did the strangling, Derek used a kitchen knife to stab her. They're both on the hook."

"Why would he go along with it?" Joey asked.

Detective Doyle looked at him darkly. "He hasn't told the whole story to us yet, but there was an...incident involving the two of them and a classmate back home. Sexual assault, supposedly done by Derek, but the charges didn't stick. Abigail knows about two others. When those are proven, he'll go down for all three, hopefully."

"How could she cover for him like that?" Penelope asked, her stomach turning.

"You got me," Doyle said, a sour look on his face. "But she held it over him, got him to do things. He's given a statement, confessing to the murders and her role in both."

"When Abigail found them together, she snapped. I get the feeling he did a lot of things behind her back but with Cassie, that was the last straw. The victims back home were Abigail's friends too. Coupled with Cassie taking the spot Abigail wanted in dance troupe...she snapped."

"I can't believe they're putting on a show right now," Joey said, shaking his head.

"I don't know what it would take for them not to," Penelope said.

"What was all that business about Armand dropping someone?" Doyle asked.

"It's in the ledger for that year, 1975. Many of the photos are missing because it was an abbreviated year. She was injured in a fall, some blamed her partner, Armand. He did not dance again after that but took over the management of the theater."

"Was it Abigail who attacked Armand and the light tech too?" Joey asked.

"It would have to be," Penelope said.

"Unless it was the Bainbridge ghost," Joey said. Penelope rolled her eyes at him.

"The real Bainbridge. Gabby. Mother...why would she kill Mother?" Joey asked.

"Mother figured out Cassie's true identity," Doyle said.

"The names on the business card," Penelope said with a nod. "Connor and Chadwick...are not the same person. She recognized Cassie."

"Mother and Abigail's grandmother went to nursing school together. Mother was a nurse in Vietnam."

"The medal I found," Penelope said, "was hers all along."

CHAPTER 67

Up in the suite, Penelope and Joey sat at the main table and waited for Arlena to finish her phone conversation.

"Problems with the new assistant?" Penelope asked when she hung up.

Arlena sat down and spun the phone around on the wood in a circle. "Did you send that paperwork to the accountant yet?"

"No, I was going to drop it in the mail on the way home," Penelope said.

"Don't," Arlena said. "She can't come in today because she has an audition, something she can't pass up."

Penelope crossed her arms over her chest and kept her face neutral. "I might have someone for you to consider hiring."

"Really? Well, bring them on," Arlena said.

Penelope pulled out her phone and typed the word "pickles."

The door to the suite opened and Sybil entered with the kids, all of them carrying large shopping bags from Steiners.

"There you are," Sybil said, setting down the packages. She knelt down and riffled through one, pulling out a box. "I got something for you."

Arlena looked behind her and then back at Sybil. "For me?"

"Yes, dear," Sybil said, handing her the box.

"It's not Christmas yet," Arlena said.

"Oh, go on and open it," Sybil insisted.

Arlena carefully removed the top of the box and pulled out a t-shirt. She held it up and laughed. "I love this." The shirt black with big block letters that read: Director. In Charge.

"I saw it and thought of you," Sybil said. Arlena tucked the shirt back into the box then went to Sybil and gave her an awkward hug.

Penelope went into the bedroom of the suite and found Jackson and Dakota on the bed. Dakota was singing to herself and twisting a strand of her long hair in her finger. Jackson stared at his tablet, pretending not to notice Penelope.

"Jackson," Penelope said.

He sighed and set the tablet down on the comforter next to him. "Yes?"

"I'm going to ask you a favor," Penelope whispered.

His face grew serious and he sat up to face her.

"Stop sending gossip about the family to Candy MacNamera, okay?" She flicked her eyes to Dakota, who wasn't interested in their conversation.

Jackson began to protest, then relented. "Okay," he whispered back.

"Your mom is very happy with Randall," Penelope said. She placed a hand on his knee and squeezed. "But she's always going to be your mom first. That's how it works. She loves him, but she'll always have a special kind of love for the two of you."

"I know," Jackson sighed. "I just want things to be like they were."

"We can't keep things from changing, buddy," Penelope said. "But you know what? Change can be really amazing."

"I guess you're right," Jackson said.

"Also," Penelope said, "I'll get to see you guys all the time. And we can have some epic ice cream sundae parties up at the house."

Jackson smiled, the first one she'd seen in a long time. "That sounds cool."

"Great," Penelope said.

Jackson hugged her, then laid back down and picked up his iPad.

CHAPTER 68

Penelope entered the station and waited for Doyle to come through to the reception area to meet her. The front security booth had been decorated with red and gold garland, and a few Christmas balls were hanging from it.

"Penelope," Doyle said, leaning out of the door. "Come on back."

"Thanks for calling," Penelope said as she settled into the visitor chair. "What did you want to show me?"

"Since you were so helpful with the business at the theater," Doyle said. "I thought I'd do you a favor and take another look at my partner's bottom drawer file."

"You're investigating Richard Sotheby's murder?" Penelope asked.

Doyle leaned back in his chair and reached for a manila folder behind him. "Well, looking into." He set it down on the desk and motioned for her to open it.

The same wedding photo Mrs. Sotheby had framed and put over her fireplace was in the file, and a series of reports, interviews, notes and lists.

"A double homicide gone cold," Doyle said. "They're not the easiest to crack."

Penelope read through the suspect list, not recognizing any names at first. "Wait...Aaron Beckwith?" She pointed at an entry halfway down the list of a dozen names. "I've heard of him. He was connected with Arlena's grandmother somehow."

"He owned the building the bodega was in," Doyle said with a nod. "His company owned several of the buildings in Midtown at the time, still do."

"Why is his name on the list?" Penelope asked.

"He was questioned because the crime happened on his property," Doyle said.

"Was he ever involved in anything...shady?" Penelope asked. She thought about Ruby's death, reading about her fragile final days, in love with a powerful married man.

"I mean," Doyle began. "I don't know of any developers that don't rub up against the...let's say more shady characters in our city. It's hard to keep away from organized crime doing that kind of business. You got your contractors, union guys...you know."

"He would've been quite old by the time Mr. Sotheby was killed," Penelope said with a sigh. "Maybe someone else on here..."

"That's a copy," Doyle said. "For you to take. Anything confidential has been redacted, but it's not much. Like I say, it's an old case."

"Thanks," Penelope said.

"I know there are groups, online like," Doyle said. "True crime bloggers, who talk about these kinds of cases. I know you like to poke around in things. I think this is safe enough for me to go ahead and tell you...maybe join up with one of those groups and see what you can find out."

"Thanks," Penelope said, surprised.

"Just do me a favor and stay out of trouble."

CHAPTER 69

Doyle walked her to the door of the station and she gave him a quick hug on the other side of the door.

"You have plans for the holidays?" Penelope asked.

"Yeah, my daughter will be home from college," Doyle said. "It will be nice to take a break with the family. You?"

"I'll be with family too," Penelope said.

"That reminds me," Doyle said. "I got you something."

He handed her a red foil envelope.

"Thanks," Penelope said. "I didn't know we were exchanging gifts or I would've brought something for you."

"Go on," Doyle said. "See you soon, okay? But not too soon."

Penelope laughed and walked toward her car, the sound of the door closing behind her. She pulled her coat tightly around her as she trotted down the subway stairs, welcoming the warmth of the underground station. Once she was seated on the train, she pulled the envelope from her bag and slipped her finger under the flap, opening it.

It was a Christmas card, a picture of holly on the front. A photograph of a woman had been tucked inside. She was wearing a ballet outfit, and was mid-twirl in a studio, a barre running the length of the wall behind her. Little girls in pink tutus copied her pose, their little feet held aloft in ballet slippers.

A note fell into Penelope's lap and she opened it. She put a hand over her mouth and read the letter.

Elspeth Connor is alive and well, living the life she dreamed of in an unspecified location. She has changed her name and chosen to remain anonymous, does not want to return to her home, which she says was abusive. The Connor family has been notified. She offered Cassie Chadwick, who she met during a dance competition, a lump sum of money to assume her identity and continue the ruse of Elspeth living a life in New York. She feels terrible about what happened to Cassie Chadwick.

Elspeth Connor is of age and is not in violation of any laws. She wanted to remove herself from an abusive home, and never thought her father would set foot in New York, and especially the Vitrine Theater, but was convinced he'd attempt to try and bring her home eventually, wherever she went. Since we spoke, she has decided to relocate again. Her current whereabouts are unknown.

The letter was unsigned, but Penelope whispered a thanks to Detective Doyle.

The train pulled into Penelope's destination, and she stood up, tucking the card, photo, and letter into her bag.

CHAPTER 70

Penelope stepped into the kitchen and smiled at Brandi, who was opening the day's mail and jotting notes in a planner she had open on the counter.

"Good to see you, Penelope," Brandi said. She looked relaxed in a black long-sleeved t-shirt and jeans.

"How are things going today?" Penelope asked.

"You know," Brandi said. "Same. Wedding planners lining up to get five minutes with Arlena. I told them they all have to wait until after this engagement party is over. I tell you one thing, if half the folks on this list of potential guests RSVP in the positive, they're going to have one big gala event."

Penelope laughed. "I think that's what Arlena is hoping for."

"Well, if that's what the lady wants, she should have it. That's my motto," Brandi said with a smile.

"I'm so glad you're here," Penelope said.

"Me too," Brandi said. "It's funny how things come along right when you need them."

Up in her room, Penelope read the email on her phone for the fifth time, then she pressed Joey's number and listened to the rings.

"Hey," Joey said. Penelope could hear a crowd behind him, and the faint notes of a Christmas carol. "Where are you?"

"I'm home," Penelope said. "Arlena's got enough footage for the moment, so she's giving the crew a break. I won't be back at the theater again, actually. I've gotten another job, and Arlena thinks I should take it. It's a big bid that I didn't think I'd get."

"Oh that's great, Penny," Joey said. "I'm not going to lie and say I'm sorry to hear you won't be down there anymore. Even though it's all been resolved."

Penelope pulled Richard Sotheby's file from her bag and set it on her comforter. "Most of it has been resolved."

"So, where's this job? You're not starting before the holidays are over, are you?" Joey asked.

"No," Penelope said. "We can talk about it when I see you later. I'll make dinner at your place."

"Okay," Joey said, relived. "I can't wait to see you. Hey, I gotta run, gonna grab this cab and head back to Jersey."

"Be safe coming home. See you in a couple of hours," Penelope said.

When he hung up she looked at the email again, the acceptance letter to the bid she'd filled out months earlier, then assumed she hadn't gotten. She stared at the location, Los Angeles, and the dollar amount next to the word ACCEPTED. It was more than three times the amount she'd ever been paid on a job, underwritten by a major production company. Estimated length of project, six months. Housing covered for her and her team. It was the kind of job she dreamed about when she founded her company.

Penelope thought about the houses she and Joey had looked at together, and about how much nicer of a home they could buy together after this job. She thought about what it would be like to marry Joey, start a family with him, and how opportunities like this one wouldn't be available to her if she had young children at home.

Penelope sighed and stood up, leaving her phone and bag on her bed, and headed downstairs to her kitchen.

SHAWN REILLY SIMMONS

Shawn Reilly Simmons was born in Indiana, grew up in Florida, and began her professional career in New York City as a sales executive after graduating from the University of Maryland with a BA in English. Since then Shawn has worked as a bookstore manager, fiction editor, convention organizer, wine consultant and caterer. She has been on the Board of Directors of Malice Domestic since 2003 and is a founding member of The Dames of Detection. Cooking behind the scenes on movie sets perfectly combined two of her great loves, movies and food, and provides the inspiration for her series.

**The Red Carpet Catering Mystery Series
by Shawn Reilly Simmons**

MURDER ON A SILVER PLATTER (#1)
MURDER ON THE HALF SHELL (#2)
MURDER ON A DESIGNER DIET (#3)
MURDER IS THE MAIN COURSE (#4)
MURDER ON THE ROCKS (#5)
MURDER WITH ALL THE TRIMMINGS (#6)

Henery Press Mystery Books

And finally, before you go...
Here are a few other mysteries
you might enjoy:

I SCREAM, YOU SCREAM

Wendy Lyn Watson

A Mystery A-la-mode (#1)

Tallulah Jones's whole world is melting. Her ice cream parlor, Remember the A-la-mode, is struggling, and she's stooped to catering a party for her sleezeball ex-husband Wayne and his arm candy girlfriend Brittany. Worst of all? Her dreamy high school sweetheart shows up on her front porch, swirling up feelings Tally doesn't have time to deal with.

Things go from ugly to plain old awful when Brittany turns up dead and all eyes turn to Tally as the murderer. With the help of her hell-raising cousin Bree, her precocious niece Alice, and her long-lost-super-confusing love Finn, Tally has to dip into the heart of Dalliance, Texas's most scandalous secrets to catch a murderer...before someone puts Tally and her dreams on ice for good.

Available at booksellers nationwide and online

Visit www.henerypress.com for details

MURDER IN G MAJOR

Alexia Gordon

A Gethsemane Brown Mystery (#1)

With few other options, African-American classical musician Gethsemane Brown accepts a less-than-ideal position turning a group of rowdy schoolboys into an award-winning orchestra. Stranded without luggage or money in the Irish countryside, she figures any job is better than none. The perk? Housesitting a lovely cliffside cottage. The catch? The ghost of the cottage's murdered owner haunts the place. Falsely accused of killing his wife (and himself), he begs Gethsemane to clear his name so he can rest in peace.

Gethsemane's reluctant investigation provokes a dormant killer and she soon finds herself in grave danger. As Gethsemane races to prevent a deadly encore, will she uncover the truth or star in her own farewell performance?

PILLOW STALK

Diane Vallere

A Madison Night Mystery (#1)

Interior Decorator Madison Night might look like a throwback to the sixties, but as business owner and landlord, she proves that independent women can have it all. But when a killer targets women dressed in her signature style—estate sale vintage to play up her resemblance to fave actress Doris Day—what makes her unique might make her dead.

The local detective connects the new crime to a twenty-year old cold case, and Madison's long-trusted contractor emerges as the leading suspect. As the body count piles up, Madison uncovers a Soviet spy, a campaign to destroy all Doris Day movies, and six minutes of film that will change her life forever.

Available at booksellers nationwide and online

Visit www.henerypress.com for details

A MUDDIED MURDER

Wendy Tyson

A Greenhouse Mystery (#1)

When Megan Sawyer gives up her big-city law career to care for her grandmother and run the family's organic farm and café, she expects to find peace and tranquility in her scenic hometown of Winsome, Pennsylvania. Instead, her goat goes missing, rain muddies her fields, the town denies her business permits, and her family's Colonial-era farm sucks up the remains of her savings.

Just when she thinks she's reached the bottom of the rain barrel, Megan and the town's hunky veterinarian discover the local zoning commissioner's battered body in her barn. Now Megan's thrust into the middle of a murder investigation—and she's the chief suspect. Can Megan dig through small-town secrets, local politics, and old grievances in time to find a killer before that killer strikes again?

Available at booksellers nationwide and online

Visit www.henerypress.com for details